A LINE IN THE SAND

Ron Rendleman

A Line In The Sand

Published by Sterling Productions
P.O. Box 41
Sterling, Illinois 61081
1-800-668-1876

Printed in the United States of America

Library of Congress Catalog Card Number 97-66514

ISBN 0-9650884-1-3

Other Books By Ron Rendleman

Tears For A King

Disciple in Blue Suede Shoes

You Can't Fly Home Again

Fistful of Dust

Stepping Into The Supernatural

Red Sky

Cover Design: Joan Vander Bleek
Cover Illustration: Gloria Rendleman

Dedication

To every person in law enforcement, or the military, who knows the gut-wrenching pain of refusing to obey an unlawful order, we dedicate this book.

ONE

Johnny Zoe drove along the frontage road of Interstate 57 through southern Illinois in his 1974 black Corvette, his attention focused on a timber ridge high up to his right. As always, he drove with the top down. He was deeply tanned with short-cropped, receding sandy hair, and he wore Avanti polarized sunglasses that gave him a youthful look.

He wasn't very big, just under five feet eight, but he was trim. At 45, he was in better shape than most younger men because his profession demanded it. He worked for the Bureau of Alcohol, Tobacco and Firearms, and his specialty was long range shooting. Up ahead on that ridge somewhere was his assignment.

Just behind his seat lay his favorite rifle in its aluminum case, a Remington 700 VS .308 bolt action that weighed nine pounds, had a free floating 26-inch barrel, and a textured black Kevlar composition stock with an aluminum bedding block that ran the full length of the receiver. The bureau had recently ordered a half dozen .50 caliber Barrett sniper rifles, big heavy brutes, but he wasn't at all interested. With his Leupold 3.5 x 10 variable scope, he could place a 168 grain bullet, that normally dropped 50 inches at 500 yards, into a 10-inch pattern at twice that distance.

He had been with the bureau nine years.

When he arrived at the first checkpoint, he flashed his ID, and driving on, passed various government vehicles and satellite dish vans of the media parked on both sides of the road. He found the designated command vehicle, got out, and stretching his lower back, looked up at the ridge. High up at the edge of the timber line was the compound, a large farmhouse surrounded by several smaller frame buildings. He could see why the bureau had pulled back to the road after being refused entry, the long sloping hill and access lane were fully exposed.

Around him, some two hundred agents of the ATF and FBI hostage rescue teams sat in various vehicles, or stood together, conversing. Most wore black jump suits, body armor and carried helmets. He approached the command vehicle.

"John Zoe checking in," he said to the balding desk-type staffer sitting at a card table.

"Zoe, lets see, yes, from St. Louis. Got you down. Sleeping tent and chow wagon are down at the other end. Pre-mission briefing's at six tonight."

"Right," Zoe said, accepting the ID card and portable radio handed him.

He walked down the long row of cars and vans looking for a familiar face. He could use a cold beer, but he doubted if there would be any around. Most of the people were from Chicago and not familiar to him. He stopped at a group of five or six younger AFT agents hanging around a pickup. He accepted a Pepsi from the one who was the center of attention.

"The way I see it," the agent was saying, "those people at Waco had every chance in the world, hell, we gave them 51 days."

"I still say it would have been better for everyone if you guys had just picked Koresh up in town," a second agent said.

"Well, hindsight is always better, you know, but it wasn't my decision, even our COs' were out of the planning early on. When we turned it over to the FBI, all the heat fell on them. Even their own behavioral experts tried to warn them they weren't dealing with a hostage situation, but a cult."

"What about these guys up there?" the second agent asked, gesturing to the ridge above.

"This is different. The way I see it, this will go down very quick and clean. These weekend marauders sound dedicated, but when they get pushed hard they'll be giving up, most of them are old men with families. Why do you think the chief isn't keeping the press two and a half miles back like we did at Waco? You watch. Harding will be operating strictly by the book, and he'll have a great example of what will happen to those militia guys when they buck heads with the government."

There was general agreement from the others, including Zoe. Everyone knew you didn't resist a law officer. You submitted to him, regardless of the circumstances; later on, you were entitled to due process. The law was supreme, especially the Federal government's.

At six o'clock Zoe sat on a hillside amongst groups of agents who pretty much kept with their own clans, smoking, chatting, and occasionally laughing loudly. They were mostly young, unseasoned hard-charging types, whose "pack" mentality didn't allow the questioning of moral issues. Their motto might easily have been, "We do not think, we obey."

When John Harding stood up, the group quieted. He was middle aged, wore black fatigues, and had eyes that darted back and forth quickly as he addressed the men.

"I'm John Harding for those of you who may not know, special agent in charge of FBI field operations. What we have here is an undetermined number of armed civilians who call themselves 'The Watchmen' and have refused our request to search the premises. Our informant tells us these people have a large amount of ammonia nitrate and a number of illegal automatic weapons. We also have information that two individuals in the group may have been involved with McVeigh in the Oklahoma City bombing. Admittedly, our probable cause could be stronger, but Washington makes the call, and the call is that we make dynamic entry as early as possible.

"We've allowed the media access. Don't be concerned, just do your job. Washington wants the country to see a well executed operation by the two bureaus working together effectively against terrorists who refuse to obey the law.

"We move at sunrise tomorrow, at approximately 0520, but be in your assigned positions by 0400. We'll give them one more chance to comply, hold off for fifteen minutes, then move in. You'll carry shields and HK MP-5 rifles only, we don't want to appear heavy handed. For the same reason, we have opted to hold back the Blackhawks and the Bradley. The approach directly up the front lane will be the least protected and that's where I want Zoe and our two guys providing long distance cover. Once I give the green light to engage, anything that moves is to be taken out. You three establish your approximate positions while there's still light today. Any questions so far?"

An agent in the front raised his hand. "Sir, what if they use explosives?"

"We pull back immediately to a safe position, but that, gentlemen, is what we're hoping for."

Some of the men looked at each other.

"It gives us the excuse to use heavy ordnance. If they continue to resist we're prepared to level the place."

There were more questions to do with details and then the meeting adjourned.

Zoe found the FBI sniper and his spotter making their way to the base of the hill. "Not a lot of cover," he said, looking up to the ridge.

They agreed. There were two or three saplings, a gully that cut diagonally across the slope, some tall grass near the road. They scoped out their positions and Zoe opted for a spot in the gully about a third of the way up the hill. He estimated the distance to the nearest building from the gully to be between five and six hundred yards. Not too tricky, if the wind cooperated. Always the wind. A long-range marksman had to know the wind, how to read the moving leaves and grass at mid range; it was referred to as reading the mirage. He saw himself lying prone in the gully, searching the buildings with the light gathering scope in the gray of early light. He saw the imagined target in a window, and as he zeroed in, concentrated on his bio-feedback, fighting the adrenaline rush, slowing down his breathing, actually willing his heartbeat to fall to 40 beats, and then, taking a final deep breath, and holding half of the next, he would half-consciously count one thousand, two thousand, and if he couldn't get the shot off by six thousand, he would abort and begin again. Such was the patience of a sniper, the supreme predator, and he neither gloried in it nor despised the killing part. It was a job, a decent living. He knew how to take and obey orders and because he was an expert he was respected, and that went a long way.

He checked out his equipment before retiring around eleven, and slept soundly for four hours. At 0345 the next morning he was in his position in the gully, lying on a poncho and taking readings from his range-finder scope. The distance to a lit upper window of the farmhouse was five hundred, twenty two yards.

At 0525 exactly, a loudspeaker on the roof of a government vehicle behind him on the road blasted, "Attention, attention. This is the FBI and ATF. We have a court order to enter your premises to do an inspection, will you cooperate?"

Harding addressed the compound three times and then it was extraordinarily quiet. Zoe searched the buildings with his scope. He could see people inside darting quickly past the windows. The sun was just coming up.

"Zoe, you read?" His portable radio crackled.

"Zoe here."

"Zoe, this is Harding. What can you see?"

"A lot of movement, sir. I see weapons beginning to appear in the windows now."

"All right. Get ready. I'll give the order over the

loudspeaker."

"Yes sir."

He lay the radio beside him on the poncho, pulled back the rifle's bolt to engage the first round into the chamber, and began to breath deeply. The sky above the compound was now a deep, vivid red. Slowly, he scanned the buildings for his first target. And then, appearing out of the shadows, a man moved quickly into the compound's big open yard, carrying something large. Zoe wasn't sure of the object, nor did he really care. He was tracking the target, the man, and when the man stopped, he put the scope's crosshairs on his head just as the loudspeaker behind him roared. "We have a green light, gentlemen, I repeat, we have a green light."

ABC's Peter Jennings spoke to the camera with the compound behind him in the distance. He was saying how the militia had just been given a last warning when the camera zoomed to inside the compound and to a man holding a large cross, when suddenly, the man's head blew apart, splattering the cross he held with his blood.

TWO

While Zoe worked the bolt action smoothly, but rapidly, firing at sure targets only, eighty FBI and ATF agents slowly made their way up the rugged incline, a long black line of faceless robotons in ski masks, armored vests, helmets and shields. They fired their automatic rifles in a continual staccato of death, but because of their inexperience in this type of assault, they were soon taking casualties from the more disciplined and accurate fire of the militia, who appeared unexpectedly from underground positions.

As government men fell, TV cameras recorded it for all America. When Harding made the recall a short time later, two agents were dead, four had been wounded.

Later in the morning, the agents reassembled at the briefing sight. Harding, not appearing too happy, stood. "Well, we had some surprises today. They have underground mobility, apparently. But no one should be discouraged. The feedback is that public sentiment is with us. Because we have taken casualties we will now move to plan B. At 0900 tomorrow we will go right up the lane with the Bradley and lobe CS canisters into the two underground positions on the extreme right.

"Zoe, can you get an angle on those ground positions?"

Zoe rose to his feet. "I'd have to be much closer. With camouflage and preparations made before first light, it probably could be done."

"Fine. I see from your record, Zoe, that you had tunnel experience in 'Nam. May we call on you, if need be?"

Zoe didn't answer immediately. Harding was so obvious with his psyche game, confronting him in front of the group, but he didn't mind, he could use a little more respect from some of the younger agents who thought him a relic. "We'll help all we can, sir," he said, and a tinge of regret hit him immediately.

The special agent in charge of field operations for the FBI then went into detail of the day's events, pointing out tactical mistakes, but he failed to mention the glaring over sight by management not to have known about the underground positions.

When the meeting adjourned, Harding called Zoe to the front. Taking his elbow, he led him out of hearing of the others.

"That was great work today, John," Harding said.

Zoe was noncommittal. He would wait for where this was heading.

"Very effective. I notice you work without a spotter."

"I haven't found a replacement that meets my requirements yet. My last partner went 10-7."

"Oh?"

"He got taken out by his wife. Used his own service piece on him."

"I see. Well, what I wanted to ask you was, on my initial green light this morning, there was a man in the yard who went down immediately. Was that your hit?"

"Yes."

"Did you notice what he was holding?"

"Not really. My field of vision was pretty much limited to his head and shoulders. Piece of timber, wasn't it?"

"What he was carrying was a cross, a very large cross. Just when he got it up, you took him out."

"Oh."

"As luck would have it, a network camera man was focused on the yard and zoomed in on the guy at the same time you fired. They've been showing that damn shot all day. I wish we would have caught it."

"Great. So the country saw an unarmed religious nut go down. Makes us look real good."

"Exactly. That's what I was driving at about having a spotter. When they have the inquiry—"

"Excuse me, but I was following orders."

"I understand, but our agency has always given the final option to the shooter—to avoid situations just like this one. I realize the ATF does things a little differently. Well, put it aside for now. The chief will handle it with Reno and the press. And I'll back you up, too."

Zoe lay on his cot in the two-man tent that night and tried to settle down. It had been a hell of a day, and he couldn't seem to let it go. The kid lying next to him didn't help either, with his jabbering.

"I'll tell you what," the kid was saying, "it got hot and heavy out there today. I almost caught it twice. I thought they were suppose to have heavy armament, but all I heard in-coming was single shots. What gives?"

"They were picking their targets."

The kid was fresh out of training at Glynco and introduced himself as Doug Kruse. He was big and still had acne, but Zoe knew he had to be at least twenty-one to have been hired. He didn't seem overly intelligent, but he acted gutsy, typical of the new breed the ATF like to enlist these days, short on IQ but very gungho.

Now he lit a cigarette. "'Nother thing. I noticed some older guys up there with gray beards. That surprised me. Who are these guys, anyway, white supremacists or what?"

Zoe remembered reading office memos describing the patriots. They went by many names, "Freemen," "Montana Militia," "Minutemen" or "Constitutionalists"—all potentially dangerous, the memos always warned. Supposedly, they had convictions that were almost cultish. Apparently, the Constitution was taught in all their meetings and was referred to as the supreme law of the land, and that was where Zoe thought they were really off. The general feeling in the agency was that the Constitution was obsolete for fast changing modern times, management never referred to it, and he doubted if any of the agents had even read it. But he had to admit he admired anyone who was willing to fight for his convictions, especially in a flim-flam society where an increasing number of people he knew, had none.

Doug was waiting for his reply.

"A white supremacist believes Whites are superior to Blacks, and if he had his way, all Blacks would be eradicated," Zoe said through a yawn.

"Oh, then how come I seen some Blacks up there today?"

"I know. I saw them. Doesn't make a whole lot of sense, but what does these days? I just do my job. White or black, far as I'm concerned, they're bucking the law."

Doug thought a moment. "How'd you get to be a top gun?"

"What?"

"Top gun, you know, sniper."

Zoe bristled momentarily. "Top gun sucks. Even sniper is a misnomer. Precision rifle shooter is more like it. "

"Sorry. How could I tryout for something like that?"

"You have to have a lot of patience, you never get in a hurry. A lot of guys can't handle it."

"I could handle it. My dad had a farm in Iowa. Sometimes I'd wait all day up in a tree stand for a deer to come through the woods."

Zoe smiled to himself.

"What else would I have to know?" Doug asked eagerly.

"You have to be a damn good shooter before they'll even consider you."

"I'm a good shot."

"Have you qualified as expert marksman?"

Doug took a drag on his cigarette and blew the smoke in Zoe's general direction, which didn't help things. "No," he answered a little humbly.

"Also, you have to be in top shape. Booze is okay, but once in a while, not every night. Good reflexes, muscle control, stamina, these things you got to have."

"They ran us hard at Glynco. They said the agent of the future had to train like a runner, I had one of the best times for the mile and—"

"A precision shooter can't smoke," Zoe continued, undaunted.

"Never?"

"Never."

"How come?"

"Figure it out. Smoke, or a smoker's cough, can betray your position and even if you didn't smoke on a mission, not smoking makes you nervous and irritable, which would cripple your efficiency."

"I can quit. I did it before."

"I see you use glasses. They're a liability. If you have to use them to shoot and you break them, you're obviously useless. They also reflect light and can reveal your position. Then there's the learning part. You got to know ballistics, ammunition types and capabilities, opticals, radio procedure, map and compass reading, and intelligence gathering, just to get started.

"But the hardest thing to learn is mastering total mental control under duress. You must be able to kill the enemy calmly and deliberately, you can't be a push over for anxiety or remorse. Young guys have a hard time with that. If you can't control your emotions, you can lose your life, or compromise the health of people you're working with. You heard enough?"

"Yeah, I guess," Doug said sheepishly. "It's a lot to think about."

It was getting late and Zoe was weary from the conversation. "Well, guy, maybe we should turn in, what say?"

"No problem." Doug snuffed out the cigarette and rolled over to face the other way.

Zoe lay looking out into the darkness through the front slit in the tent and listened to Doug's breathing grow deeper, until he was snoring softly. It would be a dark night. Clouds had moved in around sundown and he was glad. He didn't need the moon to blow his cover when he made his preparations.

He had noticed there were no spotlights mounted in the compound, and he knew the power had been cut by agents during the day. He hoped the militia didn't have a surprise like a portable generator, or infrared capability. During the day, the agency had trucked in search lights, but they would be kept off to allow him and the other shooters to establish their hides. He went over a mental list of things to do when he awoke. Everything he would need—face paint, Ghillie suit, fingerless gloves, he had already removed from his bag. He had refilled his clips earlier with his own 168 grain match grade ammo. The newer guys made cracks about his bolt action .308 because it was so much slower than an automatic, until they saw him perform. He had tried other weapons, but he just couldn't get the accuracy so important to have at six hundred yards and out. No one, absolutely no one in the entire ATF or FBI, could touch him in long range work. He was king at his trade.

But tomorrow—tomorrow things would be different. Tomorrow he would have his hands full avoiding incoming fire. Camouflage could only take him so far. The gully nearer the top ran almost parallel to the compound, giving him some mobility, but still, he was not overjoyed. He began to think about Harding's words. He didn't particularly like the manager's implying that because he didn't have a spotter he had needlessly killed the zealot.

Not that it wasn't a poor decision, he'd made better. He could blame it on being inactive for a bit too long, that he had been a little too eager maybe, but this was not the valid argument of a professional. He would have to live with his decision. Still, he didn't relish being in the center spotlight of an inquiry.

He'd been around long enough to understand the program—management makes a bad decision, then passes the buck down the chain of command to a patsy. But first, they would try to lie their way out and get Internal Affairs to confirm their lie as being "gospel truth."

Every man in the agency knew of the gargantuan pack of untruths management of both agencies told to cover their actions at Waco. He cringed when he caught some of the testimony on TV given under oath to Congress that the ATF had been "ambushed" and not fired first.

The consensus was Koresh should have come out. But burning all those kids—that really got to him. None of his friends in the agency really believed Koresh started the blaze.

He had thought about it a lot. He wondered what he would have done in Koresh's place. Little wonder the man didn't want to surrender with no guarantee of personal safety. After all, incoming high caliber bursts from helicopters was not the most ideal way to be awakened on Sunday morning. Koresh must have known all about the government's ambush of the Weavers' at Ruby Ridge, too, which would have made him even more mistrustful.

In the early days, Zoe believed in his managers. But then he saw a developing trend. Men were being promoted because of who they knew; and some promotion hungry managers would cut corners and compromise their people, allowing neophytes like Doug to get into a firefight like this one, only too willing to sacrifice them on ill-advised operations.

More than once he had been tempted to go back into civilian life, especially after Waco. He could always make a living as a hired "top gun," as Doug put it, to some country, or even the CIA, but then Magaw came in and he saw a ray of hope. The new director insisted every agent read the Treasury's Blue Book critical report of Waco, he started pushing for refresher training of agents, similar to the Secret Service's agenda. A new Treasury review board made up of ATF officials, the Customs Service, Secret Service, and Justice Department now monitored the ATF's more sensitive undercover cases.

The morale of the agency seemed to improve. The only fault he could find with Magaw was his rehiring of Chojnacki and Sarabyn, the Waco raid leaders. Putting them back on "because of their long years of service," as per Magaw, sent the wrong message to the public, in his opinion, but just as important, to the whole agency. Time would tell. For now, he would wait it out and follow his orders faithfully because of his integrity and training. Still, it was possible he was presently in the middle of another Waco. And what if these patriots, indeed, had been involved in the Oklahoma City tragedy? In his opinion no retaliation would be too severe.

He recalled some of the faces that had gone down earlier that day under his fire. One especially stayed with him—the lean one with the manicured beard, the religious zealot, standing foolishly in the open. Why had he deliberately exposed himself? What was his message? Why were these patriots so willing, apparently, to sacrifice their lives for their cause? He didn't buy all the agency or media propaganda, he learned that lesson long ago. There were a lot of questions, but he was better off letting it go. A guy could go nuts.

Something worth worrying about was that if these people were so committed, they would have to be flushed out from underground and no one knew how extensive their tunnels were. Harding would ask him, in front of the others, of course, to lead the assault team. And of course, he would comply, even though at 45, he no longer craved that kind of excitement, to put it mildly.

When he was finally finished with 'Nam he never imagined he would ever have to go down into a tunnel again, especially in his own country. It was the toughest work he'd ever done. Armed with a pistol, knife, and a flashlight, never knowing what awaited him, whether a grenade, a punji stake, or a blade through the groin; fighting fear, searing fear, that threatened to paralyze him or trick him into making a fatal mistake, he had gone down too many times.

He had looked forward to his first tour's end and getting on that "freedom bird", but then at the last minute, volunteered for another stint. Deep down he knew why. He was a junkie for excitement in those days.

He lay a long time listening to the crickets serenading and waited for sleep to come, and when at last it did, he dreamed. He dreamed about the tunnels of Cu Chi.

THREE

The dream was always the same and it usually occurred after a really stressful day. The voice he would never forget was always the beginning of it—intruding into his world abruptly, demanding immediate compliance.

"Sergeant Zoe, get your people ready, the 25th found another hot one." The Exec stuck his head into the door of the tin-roofed hooch. "Lift off's in twenty minutes."

Zoe sighed and carefully put the letter away he had been trying to finish to his folks for the past week. Another panic call from the 25th, the sixth in two days. His team needed rest.

"Lou, Pete, you guys hear?" he yelled at the men in the bunks behind him. "Time to haul ass."

"Yeah, yeah," they said, their voices muffled.

On schedule, Zoe and his squad of six tunnel rats climbed into a Huey to be air taxied to an area known as the iron triangle, twenty some miles outside of Saigon.

Zoe's team had been called to work the area almost

nonstop for the past two weeks. Most of the holes had been "cold", but each one discovered had to be painstakingly checked out, which meant another eroding attack on the nerves.

Zoe had come to respect the Viet Cong for their tenacity. There was nothing soft about them. They taught their youth, many hours each week, but they had to do little convincing. While the Americans had only a vague idea why they were there, the Cong had been fighting foreigners for years. They'd seen their villages burned out with napalm, loved ones killed or tortured by a government funded by the United States. Without air power, much artillery, or high-tech ordnance, the Cong redefined the ambush, the hit and run, the close-in encounter, getting so close to the enemy, at times, that they were protected from air strikes or shelling.

Zoe didn't agree with the Communist philosophy, but he knew the reasons the Cong had won out in the end was because they were more dedicated and their training was based on the precepts of Mao Zedong. The Communist leader had written: "The basis for guerrilla discipline must be the individual conscience. With guerrillas, a discipline of coercion is ineffective." A man didn't live underground with rats and bad ventilation and disease for years, living on little more than rice, unless he was motivated, very motivated.

The tunnels of Cu Chi had evolved from the Viet Cong warfare with the French. Aircraft, bombs, and artillery had forced the poorly equipped and mostly local guerrillas to go underground and develop a tunnel network that eventually stretched from Saigon all the way to Cambodia, hundreds of kilometers of conduits connecting villages, districts, and provinces. Hospitals, meeting rooms, living quarters, munitions factories were all underground.

The 25th infantry division from Hawaii had unknowingly built their headquarters at Cu Chi, including air conditioned offices, ice machine plants, golf courses, even swimming pools, right on top of a huge tunnel complex. The 25th were taking casualties at night and believed the cause was solely the incoming mortar rounds, until someone spotted a VC slipping into a hole inside the perimeter. Soon after, a call went out for volunteers for tunnel work and Zoe jumped at the offer. Trouble was, no one had any experience with this type of warfare, so one learned quickly what to do to survive.

Zoe found out the reason the 25th hadn't caught on any quicker to the underground system was the intricate trap doors. They were painstakingly camouflaged and were made with laminated vertical and horizontal boards and sponge rubber and were beveled downward to withstand substantial surface pressure. Zoe's squad became experts at finding them and were often called to help other units.

Now he sat in the Huey of the First Cavalry and studied his men. He was worried about them. They were all stretched to the tearing point, which meant mistakes were inevitable. They were a different breed, these tunnel rats, very prideful at being the best. All had been wounded at least once, but they were proud of the fact that their squad was still intact. They wore a badge over their breast pocket that read "not worth a rat's ass" in pig latin. They were all small men, wiry and lean by necessity, and though they verbally abused their team mates often, they had deep respect and love for one another. Other units called them "crazies," after all, no sane person would go down into a black stinking hole all alone, never knowing what awaited.

Often they were confronted by cat-sized rats, small deadly green bamboo snakes, scorpions, fire ants, and tiny organisms that got under the skin. Sometimes, spiders swarmed over a man until his body was covered with them and he would do anything to get back up in the open air away from them, often never to return below.

The Huey made its low descent to an open field on the edge of a village. As usual, the team traveled light, carrying only pistols, bayonets, and some rope, a few grenades and rations. When the Huey touched ground, the team grabbed the gear and climbed out. They were met by a sergeant of the 25th.

Zoe shook with him. "What's up?"

The sergeant, freckled and beardless, tried to light a wet cigarette. Zoe figured him to be all of nineteen but probably well seasoned, judging from the way he carried himself. "We were on a sweep when these hamburgers ambushed us back down that road. We followed them to this village when they disappeared in this field. One of our guys found a tunnel entrance, threw down a grenade, then went down, but Charlie opened up from below. We got him out but he had bought it. One of our best guys—" he paused and looked off into the distance.

"Yeah," was all Zoe could say.

The young sergeant took a long pull on his cigarette. "I'll show you what we got." He lead the squad to an area on the edge of a tree line and to a hole in the ground. The door had been blown away exposing an opening ten foot deep and barely two feet square, the acidic odor of explosives was still in the air.

Zoe had already determined to go down first. He was jumping a turn or two, but the hole looked "hot," and he didn't want any screw-ups.

"Okay, where's the rope?" he asked, and someone provided a swiss seat, a cradle of straps, in which he could be lowered into the hole. Some of the men of the other unit stood around, admiration showing in their faces.

"Let's try the drop," he said. Hank and Valdez, two of the strongest on the team, stepped forward. He took out his .38 and got into the stirrups. The drop was a maneuver he had invented. Three feet from the bottom, on his signal, the men would suddenly release him. Hopefully, any VC waiting below would be surprised by his sudden appearance, giving him a split second advantage.

"Get ready to throw down another pistol if I need it," he whispered while he was lowered. The rule was, you fired only three rounds. If you emptied your gun the VC would know it by counting the shots. He was extra careful not to rub the sides of the shaft to avoid knocking clumps of dirt loose, which would betray his arrival. He felt more wired than usual, sweat poured into his eyes and he was breathing in little gasps. A fleeting thought hit him that he was really pushing the envelope. He struggled for control, but the panicky feeling only increased as he neared the bottom.

In his mind's eye, he saw the enemy slouched against the tunnel wall, his AK-47 on full automatic. It would take merely four seconds for 20 rounds to rip into his body, so his first shot would have to be to the face, the no reaction area, since a body hit would not stop the VC from firing.

Three feet from the bottom, he took a deep breath, hand signaled for the drop and landed, pistol blazing.

The first shot went into the VC's right cheek, the second into his neck, the third and fourth were chest shots, he wasn't sure of the last two, but he kept squeezing the trigger on the empty chambers. The men above, hearing all the shots, dropped another loaded .38 down the shaft. Zoe stared through the clearing smoke, not believing what his mind had insisted on. There was no enemy, just a tunnel wall about eight feet away with his shot holes mockingly visible. He had committed the unpardonable sin for a tunnel rat, emptied his gun at a nonexistent enemy.

Humiliated by his mistake, he stubbornly willed himself to settle down. He picked up the .38 and reloading his, called Valdez down for backup. Holding his flashlight in his left hand against the ceiling to minimize his target area, he crawled forward. The tunnel was very narrow and he took his bayonet and gently probed the floor, sides, and ceiling for telltale booby trap wires. He moved very slowly, using all his experience and knowledge.

The air was heavy with cordite smoke and smells of urine and feces, and worst of all, rotting rice. He desperately needed good air, but he kept inching forward, Valdez close behind.

When he was almost to the first turn, he stopped and listened. From experience, he knew the tunnel would zigzag every so often to allow for hiding places and minimize the effects of a grenade or weapon fire.

Sometimes a pool of water turned out to be an elbow trap designed to stop CS gas from going further into the system. The water always stunk and he would have to go into it and up the other side.

While he waited, he exercised every bit of his senses. He listened, he sniffed, he felt; if the enemy were there waiting around the corner, he needed to know. Slowly, he advanced to the turn and found what he had suspected—no one.

He continued forward a few feet at a time, probing with his knife, when he felt something. He had found a trap door. The tunnel had widened enough for Valdez to crawl up beside him. While his teammate held the light, he took his knife, found the cover's edge, pried it up quickly and fired three shots.

Before he could drop the cover he saw a grenade come flipping out. Valdez saw it, too, and both men dove to the safety of the turn behind them. Zoe had gotten most of his body around the corner when the deafening roar of the blast erupted and he immediately felt pain in his legs. Valdez, not as quick, caught more of the blast, and lay moaning.

"How bad?" Zoe asked.

"Bad," Valdez gasped.

"Can you grab my belt? I'll get you around the corner." It hurt like hell, Valdez hanging on to him, but somehow he muscled him to relative safety.

"Okay, rest here. I'll go back for the rope."

Fighting the pain in his legs, he crawled back to the entrance for the rope. When he got back to Valdez, he slipped the rope over one shoulder and gave a yank for the others to pull the wounded soldier out.

"Send Hank back," he said to Valdez. While he

waited he checked his legs with the light. He had multiple cuts, but no heavy bleeding except for his right knee—it was laid open and burned like crazy. He took off his head cloth and wrapped it tightly. Common sense told him to go back and have it checked out, but being so humiliated and outfoxed by the gook did not give him any choice but to go on.

When Hank appeared, Zoe led the way back to the fire hole. Noiselessly, they crawled up to the turn. Zoe peeked around the corner and could see the hole through the standing smoke. He was sure the enemy was dead, or long gone, but just in case, opted for a grenade—something, he realized, dismally, he should have done the first time. He pulled the pin and taking aim, rolled it toward the opening. It went off just as he made cover, and he knew from the muffled sound he had hit the hole.

They crawled up to the hole's edge and shined their lights into the smoke of another empty tunnel.

The rule he had insisted on for his "rats" was that the point man was changed after each trapdoor, so great was the stress, but Zoe pushed past Hank and wiggled down through the hole and into another tunnel just like the one above. Repeating the whole tedious process of probing for booby traps, he inched along until he noticed blood spots—the enemy had been hit.

Then suddenly the trail was gone. He shined the light all around and found the thin edge of a board above his head of a trap door. He tried to lift the door, but even with Hank helping, it wouldn't budge.

"I'll bet that gook is sitting on it," Hank whispered.

"Or he's hurt bad and can't go any farther," Zoe whispered. There was nothing else to be done but pull out and let the demolition team of the 25th set their 40-lb. cratering charges.

Zoe sat in the shade with his back against a giant frond tree while the medic tended his wounds. Valdez's legs were pretty banged up, but he was sitting up and smoking while they all waited for the Medivac chopper. No one mentioned Zoe's blunder at the tunnel entrance. They had too much respect. He spent the next three weeks in the hospital.

The day before he was released, a Captain Zelesky from Bravo company paid a visit. Zoe liked him immediately. His hair, cut flat top, was graying at the temples, and his clean pressed shirt was stretched by well developed chest and arms. He came right to the issue.

"My orders are to put together a sniper team and start a school, similar to what the First Marine Division have at Hill 55. The VC are making monkeys' out of our people. We go into sweep an area that's loaded with them and they disappear. We leave and its business as usual. Our plan is to set up sniper teams in the surrounding hills as a blocking force."

"They're using tunnels."

"No doubt. But I don't need you for that. You've got a reputation for being the best in probably the most dangerous work over here. And I see from your record you made expert marksman. I need people who can concentrate under extreme stress, and when they look through a scope and see the enemy's eyes, they can still kill him.

"You use scopes?"

"Unertls', mounted on Winchester 70s', accurate out to 1,000 meters, even more."

"That's over a half a mile!"

"You got it." The Captain picked up a hard bound case he had set down when he first came in. He put it on his lap, and opening the case, removed a new 30-06 bolt action Winchester. Zoe accepted the weapon, looked through the scope, and gently rubbed its oiled walnut stock. He was a sucker for fine equipment. The piece he held felt heavier than his M-14 which looked like junk in comparison.

"You've only got 60 days left," the Captain said. "You'd have to sign up again. As bad as I need you, I'm not going to give you a sales pitch. You've already paid your dues. But I can promise you this. You'll be in an elite outfit. You'll report only to the CO and you'll probably kill more hamburgers in 30 days than you have in the last year."

Zoe stroked the rifle. He was still vengeful about getting wounded and mad about his performance in the tunnel. The powerful life taker he held would enable him to play God for one more season.

He looked at the Captain, then back to the rifle he held, and then down at the case in the Captain's lap.

"I got a name for our outfit, Captain. 'Murder, Incorporated.'" And he never dreamed he had just coined a phrase that stuck with the snipers for the duration of the war because they carried their weapons in special hard bound cases.

FOUR

His wrist watch alarm went off at 0400. He awoke immediately and lay for a few moments listening to Doug's snoring. When he crawled out of his sleeping bag, he found the air had turned much colder. He threw on his fatigues quickly, then the Ghillie suit and cap, specially made with hundreds of long strips of dangling brown and green burlap that would break up the outline of his body and make him appear in an open field like a pile of dried weeds. He put camouflage paint on his face without a mirror.

When he was satisfied he hadn't forgotten any thing, he moved quietly down the road toward the compound. Total darkness and a heavy stillness held the night. He began the long crawl up the hill, his progress impeded because he could not chance using his light. He stopped every few feet to listen. The compound was blacked out. He scanned with his night scope but found no evidence of infrared being beamed. Approximately two hundred yards from the crest, he discovered the gully he had spotted in his scope the day before. Apparently caused by erosion, it appeared about two feet deep. Bushes here and there made it an almost decent hide. He was much too close, but it was the only way to get an angle on the underground positions. He liked the flexibility he would have to move up or down the gully, because in his business, one never fired more than two or three times from the same position.

When he had everything ready, he found a tolerably comfortable position on his back in the gully and began the long wait. The cloud cover started breaking up. He could see a star or two and it reminded him of all the times he had lain for hours on hot summer nights studying the constellations. He had camped out a lot as a kid, always by himself, and knew most of the state parks in Illinois and Iowa. His dad's farm in Illinois was only 30 miles from the Mississippi. He had promised Dad he would stick around when he got back from 'Nam, and he did try, no one could deny it. But then the old feelings returned.

"How long will you be gone this time?"

"I don't know, Dad."

"But you just got home." The elder Zoe had been shoveling spilled corn off the floor. He straightened up and squinted into the sun setting behind his son, his deeply creased face betraying his disappointment.

"You know, son, your mother and me could hardly wait for you to get back from the war. It was all I could do the two and a half years you were gone to keep this farm going. You figure on doing any farmin', ever?"

As they walked together to the house, Zoe searched for the right words. The last thing he wanted to do was to hurt his dad and mom. He was their only child and a surprise when he had come to them so late in life. He knew they were counting on him.

"I honestly don't know," Zoe said.

When they got to the house his dad went to an old refrigerator on the screened in back porch, took out two cans of beer, and handed one to his son. The two men sat down in old rattan chairs and watched the sun slowly slip behind a hill.

After a time the elder Zoe cleared his throat. "You know that rock overhang up there?"

"Sure," Zoe answered. He had ridden his bike to the rock as a kid countless times. It had a great view of the surrounding country.

"Years ago, before people had cars or trucks, they'd rest their teams up there and maybe eat a snack on their way to town," the elder Zoe said. "One time a couple of men stopped up there, a father and his son. The father was up in years and pretty trembly. Winter was coming on and the son was concerned, there would be precious little to feed his wife and baby and himself. They were very poor, and the drought had spoiled the crops.

"The day was a bit bitey, but the men had blankets for their legs and the sun warmed their backs, so they sat there on the wagon and shared the hard cider the old man had taught his son to make. After a while, the son said, 'Paw, I've been fretting about the way you've been ailing lately, I'd feel a lot better if I knew you'd be in a warm place with plenty of vittles and someone to look after those old bones. Do you think you'd like to stay at that county home in town for a while?'

"The old man's filmy blue eyes looked questioningly at the boy. 'The poor house?' he asked.

'Some folks call it that, I suppose,' the son answered.

"The old man buried his head in his arms and didn't say anything for the longest time. It's true the son had given his word it would never happen, but he had no choice, don't you see?

"After a moment, the boy gleefully slapped his father's knee. 'I heard they got a light bulb at that home that warms your bones just like the old sun, suppose to make a new man of you. Why, come spring when I fetch you home again, you'll be doing the side-straddle hop.'

"For a long time the old man didn't answer, he just looked out across the country he'd been born and raised on. After a while, he turned and looked at his son. 'You'd be back by come spring?'

"'Who'd help with the plantin' otherwise?' the son answered. He had to make it as easy as he could, but he was lying. The old man brightened up some and they continued on their way to town. He rambled on and on about the molasses he planned to make when he got back, and all the time he was too trembly to even start a fire, let alone cook anything."

When his dad didn't continue, Zoe asked, "Were they neighbors of ours?"

"No. I should have told you a long time ago, but I was ashamed. The father was your granddad, Wil. It was me who drove him to town that day. He never got to go back to the farm he loved so much. He took to his bed and died that next spring. I did try to visit him whenever I could, though." He studied the floor at his feet.

Zoe sought the right words. "Like you said, you didn't have any choice, winter was coming on and—"

"I know. But I should have kept him home where we could watch him. We would have made it, somehow. Strangers can't give the same care kinfolk can. Every time I think about it I regret I didn't listen to my heart from the beginning. Always listen to your heart, son, it won't lie to you."

"Well, its done now."

"Yes."

"You worried about you and Mom?"

"Yes."

"I give you my word I will never put you or Mom in a home. Never."

"Promise?" the elder Zoe insisted, and the men studied each other, reflecting on another promise made long ago.

A week later, he was headed west on Interstate 80 in his old Bronco, the back end packed with about everything he owned. His destination was a little town outside of California's Sequoia National Forest called Lone Pine, to an address he received in the airport at Saigon.

He didn't waste money on motels, but camped out every night or slept in the back of the Bronco when it rained. He was in no hurry. He stopped often at tourist traps, or took side trips to explore historical sites. When he finally pulled into the front yard of a rundown farm house, arousing chickens, geese, and an old beagle asleep in the sun, a chubby Mexican came out of the shack wearing only Levi cutoffs and a pair of beach thongs. Valdez was a good twenty pounds heavier. Zoe jumped out of the truck and they hugged.

"Hi, wetback," Zoe said, laughing.

"Hi, Sarg," Valdez said. "You made it, huh?"

They drank beer on the front porch and watched the Inyo mountains change color toward evening and when the beer ran out, Valdez scrounged around and found pot he'd been saving for the occasion. Zoe was a seldom user in 'Nam but he was in a partying mood. Valdez's stuff was very smooth.

"So, where's your wife?" Zoe asked, looking around.

"She left. We wasn't really married you know. I found out she was laying every farmhand in the valley while I was in 'Nam. She wouldn't cop to it so I kicked her out. I miss her cooking though."

"Leg heal okay?"

"Yeah," Valdez said, looking down at the pink scars that riddled his right calf muscle. "I finally got to where I can almost walk without a limp. Hey, it could have been worse."

"You bet." When I think about it, it amazes me that we never bought the big one." Zoe took some pot and the cigarette papers and awkwardly rolled himself another joint.

"So you makin' it okay on your disability checks?"

"Yeah, I do an odd job here and there when I need a little extra beer money. The whole secret is keepin' the overhead down. I own this place, such as it is. If they don't get crazy with my taxes, I should be okay."

"You get any flack when you got back?"

"They left me alone. Those hippy protesters come around here messin' with me, I waste them. They know it, too."

Zoe believed him. Killing never bothered Valdez in 'Nam.

"How 'bout you, Sarg? You got plans?"

"Zoe took a long toke on his joint and held his

breath for a while, then exhaled slowly. "Nothing definite. My dad wants me to take up farming, but I don't know if I'm ready to settle down. Hell, I'm only twenty-three."

"Well, you're welcome to hang here as long as you want, you know that."

"I know."

So they sat and talked into the early morning about the good and bad times in 'Nam and they both hoped that the hellish nightmares they both experienced would eventually go away.

The next few days they went squirrel hunting, worked on Valdez's old jeep and visited the local honky-tonks at night, and after a week, Valdez announced he would be gone a few days. He had made a previous date with an old girlfriend in the next county. When he still hadn't returned after a week, Zoe decided to visit L.A. Leaving a note for Valdez, he headed the Bronco down Route 395.

A couple of hours later he was just heading into a town called Randsburg when he noticed a hitchhiker, a young guy with patched Levi's, long blond hair, and a nice smile.

"Where you headed?" Zoe asked pulling up to him.

"'Bout thirty miles down 395."

"Jump in."

They rode along for a while when the young guy asked, "Care for a joint? Got some good stuff."

"Why not?" Zoe answered.

The dope broke the ice between them and they chatted about women and cars, and when they got to the young guy's stop, he said, "Hey, me and my brothers are throwing a party tonight. Lots of beer, dope, women, the works. Like to come?"

"I don't know."

"You on a tight schedule?"

"Not really."

"Well, you can turn down that dirt road right there and drive about five miles up into the hills to my place and have the time of your life."

Zoe turned it over for a moment, then said, "What the hell, let's go," and he shoved the Bronco through the gears.

The young guy's name was Rick and he was right about the party. It didn't just last one night, it went on for three days, and it was a party Zoe would never forget. For three days he drifted in and out of reality, dimly aware of pretty faces and sensations. It was almost like a delayed fuse bomb had gone off inside him, and the party became *his* much overdue celebration for having gotten out of 'Nam alive.

On the morning of the fourth day, he awoke with a colossal headache. People were sprawled out all around him, sleeping. There were voices out in the yard some distance away from the house and he wished they'd shut up.

But then he distinguished a word or two and he began to listen.

"Your old man got you out of the draft, but me, I had to sweat my way out of it in a tough school. If my grades dropped they could get me anytime. I sweated through every semester."

"Well, that's one way," a second voice said. "But you should have gotten some quack doctor to write you a letter. That's all I did. We called it asthma. 'Course having a heavy chest cold the day of my physical didn't hurt either. Far as I'm concerned only dummies went to 'Nam."

"Can you imagine anybody stupid enough to enlist?" the second voice asked. Other voices agreed.

"I don't know," a third voice said, "I knew a guy who was in Vietnam. Half the people in his unit would get stoned on pot or hashish. They didn't do any fighting, just got stoned every night. Nobody over there took that stupid war seriously."

Zoe slowly got to his feet and went to the doorway. Rick, his brothers, and two other guys were sitting around a fire in the backyard.

"My outfit took it seriously," Zoe said quietly.

"Then you were a bunch of dumb sucks," one of Rick's brothers, the one with long red hair, sneered, and everyone laughed.

Zoe thought about it. He could walk away and forgive their ignorance, or he could set the record straight for the guys who couldn't speak for themselves. He made his decision, took a step forward, picked up an empty beer bottle and threw it at the speaker with all the force he could muster. It hit him on the forehead and the guy yelled and fell over backwards, grabbing his head. Moving fast, Zoe nailed the two closest with his fists before they could get to their feet. They were all much bigger, but he punched and kicked them all at least once before their buddies came running out of the house and helped get him down on his back—then the fun began.

They formed a circle around him and methodically kicked and punched him. When he would try to stand, they would knock him down again until Rick's tree limb put him out.

He awoke in a world of pain in the back of his Bronco, the sun full in his face. He was on a remote road somewhere in the desert. He lay for a long while trying to move various parts of his body and when he finally managed to sit up, he crawled to the driver's seat and started the truck.

He had no idea where he was, but using the compass on the windshield he drove south, hopefully, to the closest hospital. An hour later, a State Trooper found him passed out in a gas station outside Lancaster. The nearest emergency room was at Edwards Air Force Base, and since his ID revealed his veteran status, they took him in.

He was unconscious from drugs for two days. When he painfully awoke, both forearms were in casts and his chest was tightly wrapped. A male nurse gave him the report—severely bruised ribs, a kidney ruptured, mild concussion, both wrists fractured, multiple face lacerations.

A week later he was transferred by ambulance to the V.A. hospital in L.A. There they x-rayed him thoroughly and determined that he would not have any permanent damage.

Once or twice, he thought to call his folks, but he couldn't lie to them, so he decided to spare them from worrying. He tried to call Valdez but his number wasn't listed. So as the weeks crawled by, he concentrated on the painful therapy and a plan of revenge.

It was a month before he could even make a fist, two months before he could pick up a dumbbell. The staff bent the rules and let him use the weight room and he would pummel the heavy bag often, ignoring the pain.

At night he would lie awake and think about Rick

holding that tree limb. He was pretty sure the three brothers were growing marijuana and selling it to the local heads. He thought to put the law on them, but that wasn't his style.

Early one morning two months after his arrival, he was released. He had about seventy-five dollars in his wallet, plenty for his plan. He gassed up the Bronco, bought ham and eggs for breakfast, then headed to the nearest hardware store. He bought a piece of two-inch thick foam rubber, an ax handle and a roll of duct tape. He drove straight up Route 395 and turned off at the dirt road leading to the brothers' place.

After a short distance he found a secluded thicket, parked, and made his final preparations. First, he took out his pocket knife and cut the foam rubber in two pieces, to fit the front and back of his body from armpit to just below the waist to protect his still tender ribs and kidneys. When he was satisfied, he secured the rubber with the duct tape. He picked up the ax handle and swung it in the air to check his mobility. He had chosen the hickory handle over a baseball bat because its lightness would allow him to inflict injury more quickly in a tight spot.

When everything felt right, he got back into the truck, put both hands on the wheel, looked out at the brilliant mid-morning, and took a deep breath to control the adrenaline rush. Being habitual party animals, he knew they would probably still be in the sack. His only real concern was that some of their friends might have slept over.

Reaching under the car seat, he found the .38 he had brought back from 'Nam. It was a blued Colt revolver with a $3\frac{1}{2}$-inch barrel, well oiled and protected in the full flap holster. He flipped open the cylinder and examined the six-shot load. He was greatly tempted to slip the piece in his belt under the foam rubber for insurance, but after thinking about it, he put it back under the seat. The brothers could have wasted him when they'd had their turn, but they didn't. They just put him in a world of hurt. Now he would welcome them to his world.

Parking the Bronco a quarter of a mile from the house, he cut through the woods to approach it from the rear. He was in luck. There were only two cars in the driveway. Quietly, he moved to the back porch. A kitchen window was open. Rick was sitting at the table in his shorts drinking coffee and reading a newspaper. Zoe thought to wait until he knew the location of the other two, but he didn't want to chance being discovered. He grabbed the ax handle with two hands and crashed the door.

Rick jumped to his feet and threw his coffee cup at Zoe, just as the ax handle caught him in the temple. His eyes rolled back and he collapsed to the floor. Zoe was about to give him a couple more when a door flew open to his left and the red-haired brother stood in a bathroom entrance, his pants down around his ankles. When he saw Zoe, he tried to pull his pants up and advance at the same time, but Zoe took the handle and rammed him in the gut before he had moved two feet. The guy let out a gasp and grabbed himself. He was down on his knees when Zoe used the same thrust square in his face, breaking bone. He hit the floor hard on his face and lay unmoving. Immediately a puddle of blood oozed from his head.

Zoe examined the other rooms quickly but they were

empty. He stood in the kitchen trying to decide his next move. He was tempted to make them for anything of value, but decided against it. When he turned to leave he had to step over Rick who was on his back with his mouth open. He was starting to come around. Zoe thrust downward with the handle and a front tooth broke off.

"Eye for an eye, dude," he said, and he walked out to the back porch and scanned the area quickly for the third brother. Seeing no one, he started to jog down the road to his truck, stopped, went back to the porch and cut the phone lines.

He was in sight of his truck when movement caught his eye out in an open field to his right. The third brother was strolling leisurely along with a squirrel rifle on his shoulder. Using bushes along the road for cover, Zoe moved quickly to where the guy would probably leave the field. Zoe remembered him well, he was the fat one who trashed his wrists with his metal heeled cowboy boots.

When the brother was almost to the road, Zoe jumped out of his hiding place. "Hello, hippy freak," he said, smiling.

The guy attempted to pull the rifle down into position, but Zoe's ax handle caught him in the throat. He gasped in pain and lessened his grip on the rifle. Zoe yanked it away and threw it in the bushes.

"Didn't think you'd see me again, didya?" Zoe asked, advancing with the ax handle at the ready.

For a big guy, he could move pretty quick. He lunged at Zoe who jumped sideways and walloped him in the back of the head. He dropped to his knees and then to all fours. But before he could get his feet under his massive body, Zoe got in front of him, and holding the ax handle like a baseball bat, swung as hard as he could. The sound of cracking bone echoed through the woods and the guy slumped unconscious to the ground. As he stood over him, Zoe got an inspiration. He grabbed the guy's right leg and pulled the boot off. One quick thrust with the handle broke the big toe. It would be a while before the guy did any more stomping.

Once he started driving, he went right up Route 395, past Valdez's town, and never stopped except for gas until he got to Illinois. While he drove hour after hour, he kept going over his life. "Going Civvy" hadn't been as great as he thought it would be. His life had become little more than a endless circle of boredom, except for the party times, which were okay, but not enough to fix what he felt down deep. And he didn't like being out of control while he was high.

Maybe if he got a job he'd at least feel useful—something like long haul trucking, perhaps, but he quickly rejected the thought—he'd be bored sick in a month. He decided, finally, he would stick around and help dad, at least for the time being.

And for the next several months he did a good job of it. He got up early each day to spare dad the morning chores and worked till dark mending fences, or planting crops and tending the small herd of livestock. On some Sundays he would take the Winchester 70 Captain Zelesky told him to keep when he left 'Nam and go out and practice on the range he'd set up on a back pasture.

He enjoyed hunting a lot, but putting a grouping inside a ten-inch bulls-eye at 1,000 yards really turned him on. At first he thought it was because few other guys could do it, but he knew it was more than that. He remembered the first time in 'Nam when he nailed a hamburger leading a buffalo loaded with rifles at over 800 yards. He became an instant Zeus, hurling lightening bolts of destruction across heavens and rice paddies, alike. Few people understood it. He wasn't sure he did, totally, he just knew that rice paddy hit was one of the greatest highs of his life.

Encouraged by steadily improving scores, he began to think about getting a better weapon and enter competitive shooting, maybe even go after the Wimbledon Cup. Talk about a challenge. To be the best in the world had to be the ultimate trip. It would open new doors, endorsement offers would pour in, the possibilities were endless. So he bought a Remington 700, and in a couple of months his scores were so good he could hardly believe his eyes.

One late afternoon in September, he was coming from the field when he saw a new black Ford sedan parked at the house. He knew, without really knowing how, that it was the government. Immediately, his thoughts flashed back to the three brothers.

The guy sitting on the front porch with dad was dressed casually.

"Hi, I'm Jack Towzer," the guy said, getting up and sticking out a hand, "CIA. I see you're keeping your skills up." He eyed the Remington.

He was tall and slim, and smiled too eagerly to suit Zoe. He waited for what was next.

"Yep," Zoe said, sitting on the top step of the porch. "Me and Betsy have a good time," he said, stroking the piece.

"What can she do at 1,000 yards?"

"Most days all X's."

"Really?" The guy looked genuinely impressed. "Sure would like to see that."

"Well, come around some Sunday and we'll give you a demonstration."

Jack Towzer looked at his watch. "You know, I drove over from Rockford and I'm not sure when I can get back. Could we do it now?"

Zoe looked at him a moment. "Why are you here?"

"Fair question. Tell you what." He turned to the elder Zoe, "would you mind if John and I went for a walk?"

"Be my guest," The elder Zoe said, gesturing toward the road.

"Maybe we could walk over to your range, would you mind?" Towzer asked.

While they strolled to the range, Towzer asked. "How would you like to be a contractor for the CIA?"

"Doing what?"

They were approaching a stack of hay bales. Zoe busied himself with putting the fresh target he carried rolled up under his arm into place by punching ten penny nails into the four corners and into the bales. When he was satisfied, he began walking back across the field.

"Officially, you'd be on the payroll of a major corporation, but actually, you'd be a covert operative."

"Doing what?"

"Depends."

"On what?"

"On how good you are with that thing."

When they reached Zoe's shooting position, a carport

type shelter over a picnic table and a rubber tarp staked to the ground, Zoe took the prone position, using a sand bag to support the rifle. He looked through the scope and studied the mirage at mid-range, how it danced and boiled and tilted with the wind. Conditions hadn't changed much since earlier, the wind had blown from his left at about six knots, so he didn't mess with the scope's hairs. Earlier, he had set them by dividing the angle of the mirage by four, then multiplying the velocity times ten, which represented one thousand yards. Then he divided that again by four giving him the number of "clicks," or half minutes of angle, he would need to offset the wind.

Later on, when he thought about it, all he remembered was being a little miffed, but as soon as he locked on the target, he squeezed off the five rounds as fast as he could work the bolt.

Towzer looked at him with a quizzical look but didn't say anything while they walked back to the target. All five shots were in a six inch grouping, a little left of dead center.

"Unbelievable." Towzer said, holding up the target. "I've never seen anyone do that."

Zoe was gloating inside, but his expression could have qualified him for Mount Rushmore.

FIVE

Zoe scanned the compound with the scope, but though there still wasn't any movement, he knew the militia were probably not asleep. 0453, another fifteen minutes, or so, to daylight. Soon he would be able to examine his hide for anything that might give away his position. Then four more hours to wait in full light, avoiding movement, just waiting, calling on the discipline he learned through the years.

These patriots were hard to figure out. Taking on two federal agencies wasn't very smart, in his thinking. They had to be resisting inspection because they were illegal—to think they were standing on some principle was outlandish. Then he remembered a few times in his life when he had done just that, like when he took on a whole crowd at Rick's party in the mountains of California. That was totally outlandish.

But this was different. These renegades were thumbing their noses at their own government. Even if the agencies had screwed up at Ruby Ridge and Waco and had lied afterward to Congress, creating a lot of distrust, it didn't give anyone the right to take the law into his own hands. And yet, the older he got, the less clear the right or wrong of a situation became, including many of his more recent assignments.

When he was a kid in 'Nam any questionable action was covered by "we were following orders." Things were uncomplicated then, the government was always right. Even when a lot of guys developed an attitude about why they were over there, he didn't. But when the U.S. had pulled out 15 years later and the country was still screwed up and some sixty thousand American kids, and who knows how many Vietnamese, had been sacrificed on a political altar, he started thinking differently.

That's why he didn't waltz with Towzer for almost a year, until he was so bored farming, he had to do something—or go crazy. He made it through the CIA's boot camp somehow, intense as it was, but when instructors kept referring to President Kennedy's murder as a classic example of how to bring down a world leader with a team of shooters, he became troubled.

They showed a 16mm film and still shots of the entire episode and had information they had to be in on, to have known. They revealed four shooters were involved. One was on a one-story wing of the book depository, another was at street level, although it was never made clear whether he was on the grassy knoll or in a street man-hole. The third and fourth shooters covered two different possible routes to the hospital and were accompanied by spotters with binoculars. Their job was to finish off the President if he appeared to be alive. Zoe overheard one of the CIA instructors during a coffee break say to another, "it went pretty well in Dallas."

It was a tough call for Zoe. He loved his country with a passion and believed its agencies, though not perfect, could be trusted to always do what was in the country's best interest. Believing he might have been hasty in judgment, he decided to stick around, and by the time he received his first assignment, he'd had so much mind bending indoctrination, what was moral or proper got very complicated. "Following orders" still seemed the easiest way to go.

He remembered sitting with Towzer at the airport on that rainy day in 1975, and how unconcerned he had been when he was told he was flying to the Far East to assassinate the Prime Minister of Indonesia. Towzer had said the leader was giving the Chinese Reds carte blanch to his country, in spite of continuous warnings by the U.S. He remembered what bothered him most on the long flight on Quantus Airways to Jakarta was Towzer's last words, "Once you accomplish the objective, you're on your own."

"What are you saying?"

"You have to find your own way out of the country. Cleaner that way for everybody. Company policy is total separation. We will have no further contact after we terminate today."

"Great," Zoe said sarcastically. "Nothing like team spirit."

"You have a couple of options. You can grab a tourist or commercial freighter to Singapore, or the Philippines, or cross back over the border into Indonesia and use your cover as geologist to get back to the coast by plane or river boat."

"Why Malaysia? Why not get him in his own country?"

"The idea is to make it appear the work of a Malaysian dissenter. The Minister is on a peace mission and many Malaysians don't want the two countries to reestablish a relationship. He's visiting several towns near the Indonesian border which will allow you fairly easy access.

"You will overnight in Jakarta, take a morning flight to Sepinggan, a border town in East Kalimantan, formerly Borneo. When you arrive at the airport you'll call a missionary pilot who will fly you up to Long Bawan very close to the Malaysian border."

"What about the Remington? How do I get it through customs?"

"No problem." Towzer had been carrying an aluminum case which he now handed to Zoe. "Open it."

It was somewhat oversize for camera gear, but it contained a 35-mm Nikon and a lot of accessories deeply imbedded in foam rubber.

"Take out the rubber," Towzer said.

Zoe carefully removed everything and examined the bottom. Its design suggested rugged construction, but it was false. Its hidden release was a masterpiece. Later, when he laid the dismantled weapon into the four inch cavity, it fit perfectly.

"Getting into the country won't be a problem because of their technology. X-rays won't penetrate metal even if they attempt that, but they won't. They may open the case, of course. Since you are a geologist with an oil company, the equipment is vital to your work. Getting it back into the states will be more of a problem. I suggest you destroy the weapon before you leave Indonesia. Throw some cash into the false bottom; so that if U.S. Customs pokes around, you can easily explain it."

"Tell me about this missionary."

"Name's Jeff Bergman. Flies for MAF, Mission Aviation Fellowship."

"Why are we using him?"

"For the simple reason there's no cleaner way. There are no commercial flights to where you're headed. The government gave MAF permission to fly into Kalimantan if they would agree to do commercial flying, too. It's a great cover for you to get into the area unnoticed. He flies a Cessna 185 in and out of the villages, something of a hot dog, I take it, occasionally lands his plane by the headlights of his two cars his wife turns on for him. Farmer from Michigan before he joined MAF. To qualify for his stint overseas he had to have two years of liberal arts, one year of Bible school, and three years of Air Frame and Power Plant training, which means he is capable of tearing down his plane's engine and rebuilding it at his site."

"Sounds dedicated."

"Very dedicated. Depending on when you get there, he may ask you to stay over night because of his schedule. Watch yourself, he's no dummy. Study the file carefully in case he, or anyone else, questions you in detail about your work as a geologist."

Zoe's one night in Jakarta and the flight on Garuda, an ancient DC-6 to Sepinggan, were uneventful. Customs didn't even bother to remove the camera from the case, and the five thousand Towzer gave him, went undetected in his money belt.

He had to wait a couple of hours at the tiny airport in 100 degree heat for the missionary who eventually drove up in a cloud of dust in an old jeep. Jumping out, he smiled broadly and stuck out a hand.

"Hi, I'm Jeff Bergman. Sorry to make you wait. Had to fly a farmer to the hospital who cut himself with a parang, clearing a rice field. We'll take off first thing in the morning." He took Zoe's overnight bag and camera case and carefully stowed them in the back of the jeep. While they drove up a winding, dusty road, the missionary pumped him about news from the States.

Zoe figured him to be about 30. He had deep set eyes and was well tanned. He wore a short sleeved safari shirt, revealing developed forearms and large hands. When he removed the black baseball cap with gold MAF letters to wipe the sweat from his forehead, Zoe noticed he had thick, wavy hair.

Later, they sat on the porch of the house the missionary had built practically alone on the top of a hill and sipped lemonade, trying to keep cool, while Jeff's wife, Marcia, a little blond cheerleader type, whose upbeat attitude didn't fit her living conditions, prepared supper.

They sat down to a chicken casserole. Zoe had the first forkful in his mouth when Jeff cleared his throat and asked his five-year-old son, Jeremiah, to say grace. Zoe very quietly layed his fork down.

Jeremiah, as blond as his mom, rested his forehead on his folded hands and tightly closed his eyes. "Dear God, thank you for this day, and thank you for this food, and dear God, bless Daddy tomorrow when he and Mr. Zoe fly up north to...to...Long...Ba..."

"Long Bawan," Jeff said quietly.

"Long Ba-wan and give them good weather because you know how fast those storm fronts can come in and also, God, I don't know if Mr. Zoe has any kids in America, but if he does, please don't let them miss him too much while he's gone. Amen."

The casserole was quite tasty. Marcia apologized about the warm Kool-Aid; they were out of milk, coffee, and of course, ice. Jeff gulped down his food and said, "Well, I've got some things to get ready while there's still light. We'll be leaving at dawn and its best to get them out of the way."

"You need help?" Zoe asked.

"No thanks, there's nothing you can do. Relax and visit with Marcia."

When he was gone, Zoe moved his chair back and asked, "So tell me, what do you miss most about the States?"

Marcia thought a minute then smiled a smile that could melt an Eskimo's igloo to ground level. "McDonald's hamburgers."

Zoe smiled back and tried to think of something else to say. He looked around the sparsely furnished room. "You've done a great job putting a home together out here. How do you manage?"

"Nothing to it," Marcia said, still smiling. Then her smile faded. "No, to be honest, it's been hard at times. Jeff and I both had the wrong idea about what missionaries were all about. I mean, I thought I'd have at least one Dayak servant to help with all the heavier work and Jeff, well, he just knew he'd never tire of flying.

"When we first arrived here, they were having a drought and we couldn't take showers but once a week, or flush the toilet maybe twice a day, so we lived with a lot unpleasantness. When the rainy season came, it seemed it would never stop. My favorite books mildewed, then fell apart, the laundry wouldn't dry, but when Jeremiah here came down with typhoid, I thought sure that God had abandoned us." She took a deep breath. "But Jeremiah recovered and things got better and we sorta got lost in our work, you might say."

"It seems like an incredible culture shock to get through," Zoe said.

"It is, but we came here to serve. It is amazing, the more we concentrated on helping the Dayaks, the easier things seemed. My problem is loneliness. If Jeff is gone more than a day I start to climb the walls. I worry constantly about weather fronts that move in so quickly. All those villages Jeff flies to are in valleys surrounded by mountains. He never talks much about it, but if he waits too long before taking off, he has to circle up through the cloud cover and avoid hitting one of them. MAF has lost two pilots in Kalimantan so far. I monitor the short-wave constantly, and he guards his words, but I can always tell when he's in a stressful situation."

Zoe studied his hostess's face as she spoke and he could feel her intensity. She was something else, all right. If he ever settled down, he hoped she had a twin somewhere. Why two talented young people would give up chasing the American dream and live under such tough conditions "to serve", as she put it, was beyond him.

Jeff came in just before dark and Marcia had already set out kerosene lanterns. Zoe sat with the couple on the screened porch to catch a welcome breeze.

Still intrigued with his hosts, he asked Jeff, "How long do you plan to keep flying over here?"

Jeff sat his glass of water down. "Good question. When I first got here it was really neat, doing what I enjoyed the most and serving God, to boot. But after a while, flying over that canopy everyday began to gnaw at me. The jungle is non-stop. You go down and you buy the farm.

"But we went back on furlough after four years and were appalled at the changes in America. It wasn't so much the Watergate thing, or the stepped up porno on TV, as much as the individual rights of citizens being taken away—from increased taxes, to over-regulation of farmlands and businesses, to stepped-up gun control. Other missionaries think we're a little weird, but Marcia and I are gun enthusiasts. In fact, we both qualified for the Nationals the year before we came here. But what really got to us was our family and friends."

"What do you mean?"

"We just couldn't relate to them. It seemed they had their world, we had ours. They'd ask about our work, but it seemed as soon as I ran out of 'war stories', their interest waned. When I showed my slides in church, I found myself eliminating those that were not real dramatic. It was like competing with the 'Best of CBS.' Then I realized what I was doing. I wasn't John Wayne, I wasn't Charles Lindberg, I was just a guy who served God with an airplane. I didn't need to win anyone's acceptance, my heavenly Father had already accepted me."

Zoe cleared his throat, a little embarrassed. "So you've decided to turn your back on the 'good life' forever?"

Marcia returned from the kitchen with a dish of fried

banana slices and offered it to Zoe.

"Not forever, Mr. Zoe," she said, sitting down in a rattan rocker.

"No," Jeff said. "We'll wait to see what the Lord has for us later on. A corporate job flying bigwigs around has some allure for me, I admit."

"You'd be bored out of your mind in six months," Marcia said.

Jeff smiled and nodded. "She's probably right."

"When we were on furlough, Jeff's uncle offered him his new car agency in Marion—that's in southern Illinois—my hometown. He plans to retire and wants Jeff to have it with no investment," Marcia said.

"Sounds like the break of a lifetime," Zoe said.

"You bet," Jeff answered. "Financial freedom is something I could really get into—comfortable home on a fair-sized farm, the best schooling for Jeremiah, my wife dressed with the best of them, why not?"

"Why not then?" Zoe asked.

Jeff and Marcia looked at each other for a long moment. "We don't trust the government," Jeff said. "America has been sold out to global socialists. The citizens took their eyes off the Constitution and their Bill of Rights and got blind-sided. Small businesses in the future don't stand a chance."

They were up at dawn and had a quick breakfast of poached eggs and toast. When they were saying their good-byes, Marcia surprised Zoe with a big hug. He tried to get comfortable in the hot cramped cockpit as Jeff taxied the Cessna down the 1200-foot runway. Zoe waved back at Marcia and little Jeremiah, knowing he would not soon forget this family.

The Cessna poised at the end of the airstrip. Then its

engine screamed as Jeff pushed the throttle forward for maximum revs, released the brake, and they tore down the runway and into the cloudless tropical sky. As they banked right, Zoe could see the two below still waving. Jeff dipped his wings in salute, then began his climb north toward Malaysia.

Once the plane leveled off at 10,0000 feet and the cabin began to cool down, Jeff pulled out a map of East Kalimantan and studied his flight plan. The dense green rain forest stretched endlessly, broken only by an occasional ridge, river, or a lone cone-shaped, tree covered mountain. But as they progressed farther north, Zoe saw deep green gorges with furious white rivers rushing through perpendicular jungle walls, and far to the west, snow-covered peaks. He didn't see any place a plane could be set down safely.

Two hours into the flight, Jeff said, "Look over there to your right, that's the village of Long Gia, the only mission station in the area. A young married couple from the Christian Alliance group started a Bible school. They live right among the Dayaks." He reached for the microphone. "I'll give them a call. EZ twenty-six, Gustafson, you got a copy? This is Mike Charlie Hotel."

On the second call, a male voice answered, "Roger, Jeff, this is EZ twenty-six. Where you headed?"

"Up toward the border, got a geologist from the States on board doing some survey work."

"Copy that. We received a report of a storm moving in from the north an hour ago."

"Roger. It does look a little thick north, all right." Zoe followed Jeff's finger to a dark cloud formation on the horizon."

"Well, we'll be monitoring the frequency. Have a good flight."

"Okay. EZ twenty-six, this is Mike Charlie Hotel off and clear."

Thirty minutes later, Zoe was looking at the map, trying to pinpoint their position from landmarks through the thickening cloud cover, when Jeff said, "Oh-oh. We got a problem."

Zoe first thought it was rain, small black droplets on the right side of the windshield. But almost immediately, more appeared, pushed off into little streams by the wind. Jeff dropped the engine speed and flipped the transmitter on.

"EZ twenty-six, EZ twenty-six, this is Mike Charlie Hotel." A moment later they heard a weak signal.

"Mike Charlie Hotel, this is EZ twenty-six."

"We're getting oil on the windshield. Repeat, am losing oil. Can't tell how serious yet."

"Roger, where are you?"

"Not sure, I should be near Longberang but I don't see it. Heading, 105 degrees, I cut engine speed so I'm losing altitude. Now at twenty-five hundred feet."

"There's a new logging road somewhere near Longberang. Do you see it?"

"Negative. But I think this might be the Mentarang River to my right. Best bet would be to follow that. Engine's overspeeding. Cylinder head's starting to climb. Engine's real rough now—pray for us, I'm shutting down."

The voice on the radio kept up a steady chatter for encouragement, but the two men weren't listening. They frantically looked for a road, a rice field, anywhere to set down. Panic welled up in Zoe's throat, but he fought it off and readied himself for the inevitable crash. Suddenly his senses became superhuman—his hearing extremely sensitive to sounds of the airstream and the airframe creaking, now that the engine was silent.

The river widened up ahead. It appeared as though there was a narrow white strip along one edge and Jeff banked sharply for it. They were down to 850 feet and the strip looked to be less than a mile away. They would only have one shot at it.

Somehow, Jeff got them over the tallest of the trees that scraped the baggage pod underneath the fuselage. Then they were over the river bank. Jeff dropped flaps, did a slight slip, and the plane hovered silently like a giant bird for a moment, almost stalling. Now Zoe saw, to his dismay, that they were over an elevated part of the river bed filled with boulders. He braced himself for the first that ripped off half the cargo pod with a shrieking tearing noise, throwing the plane up in the air. Jeff muscled the nose back down and when they touched again, another boulder sheared the left horizontal stabilizer, turning them sideways. The shrieking sound of landing gear collapsing, and the airframe disintegrating, was the last sound Zoe heard before losing consciousness.

For a long time before he opened his eyes, he lay in a half-conscious condition, listening to a dripping sound in the distance. Though he felt content to stay in this euphoric state forever, the compulsion to open his eyes was strong. When he did, nothing made sense until he realized he was hanging upside down in his harness. He saw the pool of blood on the cabin roof beneath him, felt the pain, and realized his head was cut on the left side. As he struggled with his harness, he saw Jeff behind him pressed against the roof, blood running from his mouth, eyes staring wide open. The cabin had collapsed on his side, crushing him to death.

It was then Zoe became aware of the strong smell of fuel. A broken line had saturated his shirt and everything inside the Cessna's cabin. One spark from a shorted wire or metal striking metal could turn him into a torch. Fighting dizziness, he got the harness buckle open and carefully eased himself down to the roof beneath. He managed to push the door open with his legs and wiggle out, onto the river bed. He crawled over the stones to a log in the shade, a safe distance from the plane, and lying against it, applied pressure to the artery in his neck until the bleeding finally stopped.

When he began to feel stronger, he checked himself over. Flexing every joint, he didn't feel enough pain to indicate anything was broken, though his left knee hurt badly.

He looked back along the river bed. Fair-sized boulders lay everywhere, and strewn over a hundred yards, were hunks of red metal. The fuselage, with only half of one wing still attached and much of its aft section gone, was the only recognizable part.

He searched the southern sky. Dark clouds piled upward. It would be hard for a search pilot to see the ground. The missionary would have radioed their position to others by now, but whether any planes were available to do a search was another question.

He scanned the area around him. The river appeared about 50 yards wide. Since they had actually landed in the river bed, he knew he should salvage anything useful from the plane soon, in the event of a flash flood.

He stood up, painfully, and limped back to the plane. He tried to get Jeff out, but the pilot's upper body was impossibly encased with the collapsed cockpit. He took the survival kit off the back of the pilot's seat and the magnetic flashlight from under the control panel. He found the tote bag filled with sandwiches and fruit, and a thermos bottle still full of water.

He laid those safely off to one side, and making sure he could get clear in case of a shorted wire, keyed the radio. It was dead. Then he remembered—the aft section containing the battery and the emergency locator transmitter lay disintegrated in small fragments all along the river bed.

He unscrewed the compass from the instrument panel, then found the fuel-saturated maps. They were still readable. Satisfied he'd gotten everything useful, he went to the engine to drain the oil and any fuel left to use for cooking or signaling. But when he didn't find a container, he pinched off the gas line by bending it back on itself, gathered up his few supplies, and went back to the log.

He lay down and listened to the jungle sounds behind him. He wondered what monkey's meat tasted like. It was unlikely he'd get close enough to kill one. Then he remembered the Remington. He had to find it. He got back to his feet, but pain forced him to soon end the search.

He opened the survival kit and rummaged around for the antiseptic and the gauze and treated himself. He took a couple of Emperin with water from the thermos bottle and examined the survival gear. Crammed into the small box was a fourteen-inch machete, a can of water, rations, cooking kit, medical kit, a space blanket made from a reflection-type synthetic and a pair of gloves. He found a signaling mirror, two flares, a nylon rope, whistle, fishing kit, mosquito netting, pocket knife, file, compass, and an Air Force Survival Manual.

Opening the manual at random, he read, "Stay with the airplane unless briefed to the contrary. If you travel, leave a note giving a planned route (except in hostile territory)."

He laid the manual aside and scanned the opposite river bank carefully. Hostiles. Towzer had warned that head-hunting was still practiced by Dayaks in the more remote regions.

He picked up the machete and weighed it in his hand. Not much defense against savages with blowpipes shooting poisoned darts from a distance.

Turning to the blank pages in the back of the manual, he wrote: "October 15, 1975. Crashed at approximately 0930. Engine failure. Jeff Bergman, pilot, dead. Radio out. Heading on impact, 105°. Sustained head and knee injuries. Unable to travel."

He lay down again and felt the first twinge of remorse. He could die in this forsaken place, 9,000 miles away from home. The folks would take it hard. *Yeah, Dad, I did the ultimate for you. You can finally be proud of me, really proud.* He smiled cynically when he thought of Dad telling all his friends at the farmer's co-op in town how his boy had crashed in the jungles of Borneo, "where all those wild men are."

But he wasn't dead quite yet. He grabbed the machete, and fighting swarms of mosquitoes, went searching for the Remington. He limped back a way along the river bed, but had no luck, except he did find some dead wood for a fire and a better campsite.

He managed to move all the gear to the new site, whittle the ends of two sticks into points, and hammer them into the ground with a rock. Taking the nylon rope from the kit, he strung it across the sticks and to bushes nearby for additional support. He found the "space" blanket and put it over the line and fastened the ends down for a small but adequate pup tent. Even while he worked, he found himself wondering if Dad would approve of his job. "Wish you were here now to lend a hand, bless your old stony heart," he said half aloud.

Exhausted now, he lay down in the makeshift tent and after awhile, his mind wandered back to how it had been when he was young, the long hours he spent farming all through high school—all the times he wanted so badly to get his dad's approval but seldom had.

It began to rain. He secured everything inside the tent, then lay there listening to the falling rain, feeling very forlorn. He finished off the fruit and fell asleep.

When he awoke, rain still beat a steady tattoo on the tent. The luminous dial of his watch read 1:30 a.m. Perspiration soaked his clothes and his head was pounding again. He lay in the dark, tossing restlessly, and then he thought of Marcia. By now, they would have radioed her and he knew she would stay awake all night, rocking on that big front porch, listening to the short-wave from Jeff's office, worrying and praying.

"Keep praying, honey," he muttered. "I could use a

little help." He thought to pray himself, but reasoned if he had gotten through 'Nam without it, he would get through this. Toward morning, he slipped into a fitful sleep while the rain continued to pour mercilessly on his shelter.

SIX

It wasn't the bright sun that awoke him in the morning, but the sound of gurgling water and loud metallic scraping. Getting stiffly to his feet, he made his way through the steaming undergrowth to the river bank. The heavy rain had caused the river to rise considerably. It had reached the Cessna's fuselage and was beginning to drag it, and Jeff's still entombed body, downstream. He watched helplessly while it inched along, its one wing seemingly reaching out to the shore. It momentarily stopped, before the current wrenched it loose again. Then it was in deeper water and moving faster. In a few minutes it disappeared out of sight around a bend.

He had counted on the bright red fuselage to be seen by his rescuers, now there wasn't a shred of evidence anywhere. The current was swift; what was still left of the plane, along with his rifle and gear, would probably be washed miles away. He stood, staring down river, until the sun boring into his skull, and intensifying his renewed headache, forced him to return to the tent.

He rested some, then feeling he should be doing something, found the two day/night distress flares and read the instructions to refresh his memory. They were designed to put out smoke during the day and a bright light at night. Then he found the small plastic signal mirror and put it in the breast pocket of his shirt. That was one item he didn't want to lose. Next, he found the waterproof matches and the hexamine fuel tablets and the bouillon cubes and made a hot cup of soup.

He couldn't remember soup tasting any better. He sat there for a while next to his tent, half listening for the sound of an engine. When sand flies and mosquitoes attacked, he took a couple of chloroquin tablets and climbed back under the netting.

He traced Jeff's flight plan on the map and calculated he was somewhere northwest of Longberang. How far away the village they were headed for might be could be anyone's guess—maybe fifty miles. He stowed the map and took out the compass from the plane and checked it against the one in the survival kit. They read the same and he put them away. Trekking fifty miles through jungle would be a neat trick with a game knee and a head that refused to stop throbbing.

He could build a small raft and float down river until he came to a Dayak village. But he remembered the many rapids they had flown over and knew it would be very risky. His best bet was to stay here near the river, at least until he was stronger.

He sat with his legs drawn up under him, his head on his knees, beginning to feel depressed again. He thought to pray, but couldn't seem to start. He struggled with it for a while then said, "screw it", and grabbing the machete, started cutting the tall grass around his tent for a path to the river. He continued it along the river bank and kept a look out for anything edible. The heat pressed in, all but suffocating him. Swarms of mosquitoes hovered incessantly around his head and sharp pandanus leaves and barbed rattan tendrils cut his legs and arms, but finally, he found some ranbutan fruit.

He was busy eating the sweet fruit, when feeling something on his leg, he pulled up his pants and found several leeches he had picked up in the bush. They were bigger and more colorful, with yellow and black stripes, than the variety he was familiar with in 'Nam. About an inch and a half long, they were ribbon-like until they sucked enough blood to swell almost as large as his little finger. He scraped them off with the machete, but the anti-coagulant they had pumped into the "Y" shaped wounds continued to cause blood to ooze. He applied antiseptic, cut off some nylon rope, and tied his pant legs snugly around his ankles.

He dozed then, as the afternoon temperature soared to inferno intensity and when he awoke he was very thirsty, but his headache had subsided and for that he was grateful. He drained the thermos bottle, then looked out at the new view his bush clearing had caused. Actually, there was much wild beauty all around. On the far side of the river, cocoa, fan, and nipa palms glistened in the sun against a backdrop of 250-foot high mangaris and tappan trees towering from vast buttress roots. The underfoliage near him hung laden with orchids, mosses, ferns and flowering vines that thinned out rapidly deeper in the jungle because so little sun penetrated the thick overhead tree canopy.

He had always had a keen appreciation of nature since boyhood. Things that other people took for granted, such as the survival techniques used by all species of the plant and animal kingdom, intrigued him. A livid red and white plant nearby caught his attention. About two feet across, it had no leaves but drew all its sustenance from ground trailing tendrils. Five leathery petals were presently open to reveal a fire-red cup almost a foot deep with upright spikes. Emitting from the cup was an odor something akin to meat spoiling that drew insects. Its beauty was mind-boggling, its glowing center reminded him of an erupting volcano crater.

He coughed once and loud chattering erupted overhead. He looked up into the tree canopy 150 feet above and saw a family of gibbon apes swing excitedly from vine to vine. He saw multi-colored swallows and sunbirds, too, and an enormous dark bird with outsize down-curving bill—a Hornbill.

He decided he needed to get his bed off the ground to discourage ants, spiders, leeches and scorpions. He cut down saplings into various lengths, and using four longer sticks for corner supports, made a ladder-like bed, cross-tying sticks six inches apart. Then he gathered spineless palm leaves for a mattress. He put a space blanket over that, then his net and larger space blanket over the four supports for a protective canopy. The whole structure was reinforced by nylon rope tied to stakes. When finished, he stood back and admired it, quite pleased with his ingenuity.

Now he began to do some serious thinking about finding food. The river should have saw, cat, or box-fish. He took out the fishing packet from the survival kit, and cutting a slender sapling for a pole, found some grubs and tried his luck.

He fished unsuccessfully until dusk and when the mosquitoes got too overbearing, he left the line in the water, lashing the pole to a tree, and went to his tent. He made cold chocolate that only temporarily alleviated his increasing hunger. He lay on his new bed and listened to the change in sounds as jungle day suddenly, dramatically turned into jungle night. When the bush crickets became quiet, a different species of crickets began their song, accompanied by a symphony of burping lizards and frogs and bird calls.

In a matter of moments, the darkness was total. Though it had cooled some, he was unable to sleep. He lay on his stomach and looked out at the forest floor studded with tiny luminous fungal plants and fluorescent toadstools that shone ghostly green, and countless glowworms and sparking fireflies.

He began to hear sounds in the bush that didn't add to his sense of security. He made a vow to find a very strong ironwood sapling in the morning to lash his machete to. According to Towzer's brief, rhinoceroses and elephants had been hunted out of Kalimantan, but there were small panthers, bears, wild boars, a half dozen variety of lethal snakes, and apes to watch for. Like the orangutan, the shaggy red-coated ape that walked upright and grew to seven feet—he didn't care to have an encounter with one of them. He had read somewhere, years ago, of a large female orangutan carrying off a young male from a village. The man was allegedly found three days later wandering around in the deep Borneo jungle, permanently mentally deranged.

He continued to toss back and forth, hungry and itching all over. He looked at the stars above the river barely visible through the trees and felt somewhat reassured.

His family never did understand his fascination with the stars, nor did he. Maybe it was that the vastness of a star filled heaven represented an infinite freedom, the exact opposite of a life that often seemed programmed for performance and little else. Get that "A" in school. Be the best in sports. A favorite expression at home for as long as he could remember was, "I don't care if you're only a garbage collector, someday, just be the best in town."

Yes, Dad. But when do I arrive? What do I have to do to qualify for your hall of fame?

Hour after hour he lay in his jungle cocoon, thinking about the years he had spent at home and later in the military, the many good intentions, the disappointments, the rare moments when he hadn't felt continually frustrated, always striving to be the best, accomplishing much, but having to prove himself competent time and again.

Just when he was finally dozing off, he heard a movement in the jungle somewhere to his right. It was a thrashing noise, the sound of a gorilla, or a man moving through dense brush. Cautiously, he reached for the machete in the cot beside him. He listened to the sound growing louder as his heart began to race.

Not wanting to be caught out in the open lying on his back, he waited a few moments, then slowly lifting the mosquito netting, he sprang out of bed. Yelling like a charging lineman, waving the machete over his head, he rushed the jungle. There was instant reaction as whatever was there retreated, and for some time, could be heard tearing through the bush.

Since it was getting light, he built a fire to cook a small white rat caught in his snare during the night. But while he worked, he was careful not to turn his back on where he had heard the noise. When the sun rose, he cautiously examined the jungle for tracks, but the undergrowth was too dense.

He tried to think of different defenses in case his visitor returned. His best bet were the smoke-flares, though he hated to waste them. He hoped they weren't ruined by the humidity. He grabbed the line and fished a while, without results, the water was still too turbulent from all the rain.

Though he knew many jungle plants were poisonous, he tried some fern shoots growing along the bank that were very bitter, and a hairy-leaved plant he thought he recognized from 'Nam, but later gave him diarrhea. He spent the rest of the morning making more traps.

He had stopped to rest and was looking out at a sago palm, when he remembered an instructor in 'Nam who showed him how to use the palm's inner bark for food. He found a young tree and cut into the inner pith. Peeling some off, he chopped it into small pieces and boiled water. When cooked, it resembled oatmeal, and he had high hopes until he tasted it. It was like eating wet newspaper.

It came as a sound from a long way off while he was eating, barely audible, yet familiar. He froze. A moment later he heard it again, but still he couldn't be sure. Ignoring his sore knee, he hobbled to the river's edge and then heard it once more—a plane flying in the distance—to the south. He returned to the tent, grabbed the two smoke flares, then hastened back to the river and waited anxiously. But the plane never flew closer, and long after its sound had faded, he stood listening and hoping. He walked back to camp, totally dejected. The plane was probably following another river system, and he remembered, regretfully, the many he and Jeff had flown over.

Perhaps the searches would come farther north tomorrow. He had to keep thinking that it was only a matter of time before someone would find him. But what would he do if no one came, start trekking north? Possibly when his knee was better, that could be done. The next two days he spent a lot of time at the river, flares ready.

The days dragged by, their monotony broken only by frequent sudden downpours. He kept count by putting stones on a pile, and when he felt himself drifting into a mental maze, he spoke outloud to the jungle or to the gibbons that refused to be enticed within range of his machete.

One day he returned to camp, having been away for a long time looking for food, and found the contents of the survival kit strewn about. A Berok monkey scampered off when he approached. When he put everything back in place, he found the fishing packet with all his hooks and nylon line gone. Though the fishing hadn't been good, he had at least caught a few. The river continued to be too murky for spear fishing, so he was forced now to live on rodents caught in his snares, shellfish, insects and sago palm.

Each day he grew weaker. Burdened by a knee that refused to mend, he found foraging increasingly difficult. One afternoon he forgot his compass and became lost in a dense thicket. Panic tried to overpower him, but he sat down and made himself think rationally, retracing his way by watching carefully for the previous marks of his machete. He heard planes on two more occasions, but each time they were too far away to use the smoke bombs.

One day he heard something thrashing in the thicket, and suddenly, a large female sow emerged, with her young pigs. Zoe could see the pulp from the durian it had been eating all over its yellowish face as it charged him. Instinctively, he crouched and stuck out his spear and the sow impaled itself, as the other end of the spear's shaft dug into the ground. The blade went into the sow's narrow chest and came out on the right side just above the ribs. The animal shook its head violently and thrashed about, giving Zoe time to climb a tree while her young ones fled into the brush. One last grunt and she dropped to her knees, dead.

Zoe climbed down from his roost, shaken but thankful for his unexpected windfall. It would soon be dark and he was some distance from camp. Quickly, he went to work. He cut the legs off, bundled them and took them to camp. But by the time he had them stowed it was too dark for a second trip.

Since he knew meat rotted quickly in the tropics, he decided to stay up until everything he had brought back was roasted. He turned the meat on the spindle slowly by hand, until no longer able to contain himself, he grabbed off a half-cooked hunk and shoved it into his mouth. He gorged on three more big chunks. When the meat was cooked he tied it to a tree limb to discourage predators and went to bed, too tired to wash off the blood and fat drippings from himself. Sometime later he awoke and vomited the meal. When he awoke the second time, his legs were on fire. He grabbed the flashlight. Ants were crawling up his body. He flashed the light around and almost dropped it from shock. Thousands were under his tent and beginning to come up the support posts of his bed, evidently attracted by his vomitus and the pig's blood.

He didn't know if they were fireants. He had heard stories of swarms of ants devouring men, but he wasn't about to find out. He jumped from the bed, cut the rope, and dragged the meat across the ground to about twenty feet away.

He stumbled down to the river and washed himself. When he made his way gingerly back to camp, he found that his little trick had worked. The ants were swarming over the meat on the ground.

In five days all his remaining cache had turned rancid. He started foraging again, but each day usually returned empty-handed. No matter how hard he tried, it seemed he always managed to "spook" game by his awkwardness—stumbling over large snarled roots covered with slippery moss, or snapping a fallen bamboo. His shirt had long since disintegrated by the humidity, his pants were ragged shorts. He wished he could shave, his beard itched constantly.

Two more weeks passed, during which he found very little to eat. He began running a fever and was too weak to travel very far from camp. While wandering around in the forest in a half-conscious stupor, looking for grubs in an old rotten tree, he heard a plane approaching. The sound from its single engine grew louder and he knew it was low and probably following the river. He gave out a yell and stumbled through the thick bush, paying no attention to the barbed rattan and bamboo shoots that lacerated his arms, face and legs. Twice, he fell headlong into gullies, but when he reached the river, the plane was gone.

He dropped to his knees and wept long painful sobs of disappointment. He had survived for 33 days against a land that would devour him. He had endured with a strength inherited from his folks, and stubborn pride reinforced by his father's philosophy, *that which does not kill us makes us stronger,* and specialized training that insisted on achievement in spite of the odds. But now, his natural assets and training were no longer sufficient.

He lay on his face in the consuming sun and didn't resist the painful sense of defeat that swept over him. Then in the far recesses of his mind a thought sprouted, which at first, he ignored. *Why not pray*? He tried to think of an excuse like he always had before, but couldn't.

After agonizing for sometime, he finally swallowed hard and whispered, "Okay, God, I've had it. I've been kidding myself that I'd get through this somehow, like I've always been able to in the past. I'm not sure who or what you are, but if you're there—I could use a hand up."

He was down to the very last bit of strength, knowing he was losing the greatest fight of his life, when he slowly grew aware that the boiling sun and the sand flies and the mosquitoes and the gnats digging into his bare back had greatly lessened. Strength came to him and he stood up and looked around. Something had happened. Even the normal sounds of the jungle were strangely hushed. He quietly made his way to his tent and lay down. His fear was gone. He felt serene, secure. He closed his eyes and slept sounder than he had for many days.

SEVEN

Zoe changed position slightly in his hide without moving his camouflage. It was 0520 and the first rays of sun peeked over the eastern horizon, lighting up the compound. He studied the buildings carefully for signs of life from the militia but saw none.

He remembered another morning and a tropical sun that bounced blindingly off a river, making it hard to confirm what he thought he saw—men in a boat headed right toward him. He remembered the emotion he felt of at last seeing other humans. They were eight Dayaks straining and pumping their way up the river. His fever had broken, and feeling much stronger, he walked in the shallows looking for shellfish when they came around the bend. His first impulse was to hide, but he changed his mind, grabbed his spear and stood tall, waiting. How he wished he had the Remington.

They rowed right to him, beaching their long boat, a hollowed out log. He could see bundles of cloth, glass beads, and bags of salt in the craft's bottom. Small men with coal-black hair, lean and muscular, they approached him cautiously. They carried blade-tipped blowpipes and machete-like parangs hung at their waists and they wore only loin cloths. Intricately designed tattoos completely covered their arms and shoulders.

He smiled and waved but they didn't respond. They were looking past him into the jungle, apparently to see if he was alone.

"Hello," he said, still smiling and he did an oriental bow. They stopped at a distance and studied him. He wasn't sure whether their tattoos represented heads taken. He made signs, trying to explain how he had crashed. When he held out his arms and hummed to imitate an airplane, they began to laugh and the sun sparkled off the older mens' gold teeth. He kept trying.

Evidently deciding Zoe was harmless, one of them gave an order and rattan baskets were taken from the boat. They sat down in the shade and the one who had given the orders opened a large banana leaf filled with rice and offered it to Zoe. He accepted it and made a little grateful bow. He sat down opposite them and he and they watched each other eat. He quickly gobbled the rice and immediately accepted two more packets. After they had eaten, the men smoked tobacco rolled in palm leaves that gave out a strong odor.

He felt much better. It was wonderful to be able to ease the ache of hunger. He marveled that these Dayaks should have happened along the very next morning after his awkward prayer. He was mulling it over when he noticed the leader quizzically eyeing him. Zoe thought a moment, motioned them to wait, and went to his tent for the survival kit.

He gave the whistle, extra compass, and large

needles to the leader as gifts to repay their generosity. They were greatly amused, taking turns blowing the whistle and trying to make the compass needle come off north.

When they prepared to leave, Zoe approached the leader. "Take me with you," he said, humbly, pointing to himself, then up the river. He repeated it several times until the leader understood. A heated discussion developed. Two of the Dayaks kept pointing to the boat and Zoe concluded they thought they were loaded too heavily for another passenger. While the debate continued, he tried to think of something to help his cause. He took his spear and made the motion of poling a boat. He kept pointing to himself, indicating he was willing to do his share of the work. Without them he didn't have much hope.

Suddenly, the leader terminated the discussion and led him to the center of the boat. Zoe grabbed his spear and survival kit and started to climb in when he remembered the space blanket and mosquito net at the camp. He started to tell the leader to wait, then realizing they might not, he jumped in and they shoved off.

The men used their wide paddles against the strong current, making slow progress. But later in the day when they turned north into a tributary deeper into the jungle, it was much easier going. After several miles, the tributary narrowed to a water path. They paddled through nipa palms that formed a low archway over their heads. Along some stretches the foliage was so dense it was like traveling through a tunnel. Water vines they cut afforded them a drink fifteen degrees cooler as the afternoon temperature soared. Often, while they cut their way through foliage overhead, fireants fell into their laps, or into their hair, biting painfully.

Wild life became more abundant the farther north they traveled. Zoe spotted a python swimming along the shore that disappeared when they quietly passed, and a giant monitor lizard, at least seven feet long, sunning on a rock. He saw flying squirrels, smaller lizards, and snow-white birds that seemed to fill the banks, perched among vari-colored orchids and flowering trees, and numerous small parrots bright with turquoise bodies, blue-gray heads and white beaks, and kingfishers in regal plumage.

At times, they were forced to wade through shallows, pulling the boat behind. Sometimes they used poles against the river bottom, or caught a tree limb overhead with a large hook attached to the pole's other end. Zoe worked until his arms and shoulders burned, but he refused to slack off.

Late in the day they came to a huge gorge with rock faces on either side rising up at least 200 feet, and Zoe could see that a scaffold of saplings had been built over the rapids. It seemed impossible that the heavy long boat, that surely weighed close to a ton, could be lifted and pushed across the flimsy support. The leader gave an order and they beached the boat and began gathering wood for a fire. They would attempt the lift in the morning.

They cooked lizards and had mangosteen fruit they had found down river. Though everyone seemed friendlier toward him, possibly because of his hard work, when they turned in, Zoe determined to stay awake, afraid of foul play. However, in a short time the Dayaks were all asleep, and soon, so was he.

In the morning every muscle in his back and arms ached. He helped unload the boat, then pull it through the fast water to the scaffold. On command from the leader, they lifted the heavy craft up on the saplings, and though the scaffolding sagged dangerously, it held and the boat slid into the water again at the far end. They encountered other rapids as they continued north and had to use scaffolding twice more.

At mid-morning on the third day, they passed a village. The men in the boat waved to those sitting on the porches of long houses built on stilts. Zoe could see one of the men on the porch beating a long, gourd-like drum, apparently announcing their arrival.

From then on the drums never stopped and they soon passed three more villages. By the time they had reached their destination, a large welcoming committee of people and dogs waited on the bank.

Zoe climbed out of the boat and smiled broadly, but their response was reserved. The leader beckoned and Zoe picked up his things and followed him up a hill. They arrived at a complex of long houses, each appearing to be at least 300 feet long. He was led to a house with a decoratively carved doorway, while a hundred Dayaks, mostly children, followed, talking together excitedly. He wondered if they had ever seen a white man.

They walked up a notched log stairway to a veranda that ran the house's entire length where bare-breasted women, some very old, worked at pounding rice with a long mallet, or sat weaving rattan baskets and mats. Naked, dirty babies with black hair cut in bangs and huge dark eyes, stared at him. He had to stoop low to enter the house. In the dim light he was able to make out men sitting cross-legged against the opposite wall.

Apparently, they were the elders. A very thin old man with many tattoos and teeth stained black from betel nut, motioned him to sit. He and his escorts sat down on rattan mats. Children stared through the glassless windows.

The leader of the long boat crew began to report to the tattooed old man. When he went on for quite some time, Zoe examined the surroundings. The floor was roughly hewn boards three inches thick with six inch square holes cut in at intervals. Hanging rattan mats served as room partitions. But what Zoe saw in the rafters completely unnerved him. Over thirty smoke-blackened human skulls grinned down at him—guarded by long-tongued lizards. He knew he dared not betray his feelings. Most of the men were studying him, puffing hard on pipes and small black cigars. The skulls did not appear to be of recent vintage, he reassured himself.

Just then, two young girls began to distribute clay jugs to the men. Zoe was struck with their beauty and grace. Both had very long straight black hair and wore hand-woven sarongs, covering them from the waist down. They wore brass earrings and rattan necklaces similar to the mens'.

The jugs contained rice wine that was very rough going down. Zoe looked at those watching him and indicated he liked the drink, which was a mistake. He received a refill immediately.

The chief said something to him, then one of the elders repeated it—*"Dai Mai."* There was immediate reaction from everyone and a man went out.

He returned shortly with a young, good-looking lad

with soft eyes and wide smile. He walked in submissively, apparently honored to be called to an elders' meeting. The chief said something to him. The lad turned to Zoe. "Our chief wishes to know about yourself," he said.

"How is it you speak English?" Zoe asked.

"The chief is my father. When I was younger, I was sent to the classes of a government teacher who lived many days to the west."

"Tell the chief I am privileged to meet him. Tell him I am very grateful to his men for bringing me here, for I might have died."

While Dai Mai translated, Zoe related how he had survived the crash. There were gasps of surprise when he described the plane and nods of approval when he spoke of his struggles to survive.

The chief responded by standing, with the help of those near, to give a fifteen-minute welcoming speech. While the chief spoke, the wine kept flowing. As soon as Zoe would set his jug down it would be topped again by one of the maidens. The chief finally concluded with the announcement that the festivities that had been planned upon return of the traders would commence at once, that nothing should be spared, especially now that a guest had arrived.

A drum droned, accompanied by howling dogs, to announce the feast to the neighboring villages, and Zoe began to relax a little. Dai Mai came over and sat next to him again.

"How far is Longberang?" Zoe asked, trying to calculate their position.

"Ten days, *tuan*."

"How far is Long Bawan?"

"I have not been there. But some have. I will ask." He spoke to the men nearby. "They say it is at least eight days. One must go over land to another river system, then cross mountains."

"Is there an air field there?" Zoe asked.

Dai Mai asked the men. "Yes. They are very sure."

"I have to go there."

"I will speak to my father." The boy approached the elder, then returned. "He says it can be arranged, after the celebration, of course."

"How long will the celebration last?" Zoe asked.

"When the chief decides, *tuan*."

"And how long could that be?"

"Perhaps seven days. Perhaps longer."

Zoe felt uneasy. "Tell me, Dai Mai, do your people still take heads?"

"Would you like more rice wine, *tuan*?"

"No, thank you, not now." He decided to drop it. In his little talk earlier he had lied that he had come to the island with the government's blessing, and that men were probably looking for him, hoping it would buy some respect. He was thankful when large platters of steaming rice and chicken were brought in because he was quickly becoming drunk. The afternoon slipped into evening and plates piled high with roast pig and more rice were brought. The wine continued to flow, and many of the men became sick, vomiting their meals into the square holes in the floor near them. Pigs and chickens under the floor did the scavenger work.

When the assembly moved out to the veranda, the women joined the men, and the festivities became much livelier. Gongs, bamboo pipes, and guitar-like gambooses were brought out, producing music hauntingly soul-touching.

Some of the men put on panther skin vests, and headdresses of Hornbill or Argus pheasant feathers. For a while they danced, each in his own style, until there was a disturbance and a young beautiful girl, bare-breasted and wearing a colorful sarong and much silver jewelry, stood up. All eyes studied her as she took Hornbill feathers and slipped them between her fingers. She stood still for a few moments, then very slowly, her wrists dropped, her fingers arched, and she began to sway and move in a strange exotic dance, controlled and more oriental than primitive. She danced for some time and Zoe was caught up in her spell. When she finished, several young men rushed to the center, screaming, and poising on one foot while the drums beat out a faster tempo. With the other foot they described a circle, and at the same moment, threw out their muscular arms to represent a bird in flight.

Zoe was totally intrigued, knowing he was observing traditions perhaps practiced for hundreds, if not thousands of years. Dai Mai explained that each dance had a purpose—to influence *bali*, to protect one in battle or help the new rice crop grow. The spirit particularly concerned with crops was the great "creator" spirit whom Dai Mai referred to as "she."

"She?"

"Yes, *tuan*."

"Who told you the creator spirit was a 'she'?"

"My father, of course."

"Tell me more."

"There are three kinds of spirits—good, bad, and those that are difficult to predict. Bad spirits can cause one to die, or his crop to fail, or defeat him in battle. Good spirits can help one to find game, give healthy babies to a village, protect one's rice crop. One influences *bali* by giving the blood sacrifice of a pig or chicken."

"Tell me about the headhunting."

"My people believe *bali* of each person lives in his head. Taking a head gives one power. In past days a warrior with many heads was greatly honored. Before a man became a chief he had to prove himself as a warrior by the number of heads taken. Sometimes, when two would marry, the bride would insist on proof of her lover's manliness. A head taken from someone of another village usually was enough to win her."

"Didn't this practice start wars?"

"Oh, yes, *tuan*, many. Finally, the government soldiers came to each village to make a law against it."

"Tell me, Dai Mai," Zoe said, lowering his voice, "is the practice of taking heads totally gone?"

Dai Mai hesitated and looked out at the dancing in the yard below. "No, *tuan*. Although it is not often, a head is still taken. Last month a head was taken from a man fishing alone up river."

Zoe started to ask the reason, but just then Dai Mai was called to take part in the dance. Zoe sat alone with his thoughts that suddenly weren't very lighthearted. When no one was looking, he poured his wine down one of the holes and became more watchful of the men closest to him.

The dancers put their hands on one another's waists and began a snake dance, laughing and stumbling over each other. The "snake" got longer and soon, almost the whole village was dancing and laughing drunkenly while the musicians played their wild, throbbing music.

When it was over, everyone returned to fresh platters of roast pig, vegetables, pineapple, fried bananas and more wine. Children drank freely with adults, two or more using straws in the same jug. When someone fell down drunkenly, everyone laughed hilariously. Even the dogs became drunk and some had already passed out, lying on their backs, legs extended comically in the air.

The evening wore on and couples petted and copulated in the dark corners of the veranda. Some Dayaks fell asleep or passed out where they sat. Dai Mai led Zoe to a little hut at the far end of the village and explained that, because he was an outsider, he would have his own house apart from the others so that *bali* would not be angered.

When Dai Mai left, Zoe put his things in the corner of the small one-room hut, undid the machete from the pole, laid it at his side and stretched out on a rattan mat on the floor. He kept telling himself he needed to stay awake, to get up and sit in a dark corner, but the wine won out.

EIGHT

Zoe often thought about those days he spent with the Dayaks. He had learned much about a different way of life, stripped of the veneer of modern civilization. As he lay secluded in his hide below the militia compound, he recalled the most memorable experience of all that happened the very next morning after the celebration.

He had been awakened suddenly by someone shouting loudly. He jumped up and looked out the windowless opening of the little hut to see a young Dayak running through the kampong. Zoe climbed down to the ground to meet Dai Mai with blowpipe in hand.

"What is it?" Zoe asked.

"Boars. A herd will soon cross the river. Come." They followed the two dozen or so armed men who ran past them. When they arrived at the river, they found some of the herd had already crossed, evident by tracks in the mud. Half the men concealed themselves behind foliage on the bank, while others climbed into the boats and covered themselves with hastily cut branches. Dai Mai and the others spread out their poisoned darts on large leaves to aid rapid shooting.

An hour passed. The sun rose beating down on the patient hunters and the sandflies became a constant torment, but no one spoke or moved. A crested jay flitted from perch to perch just over their heads and Dai Mai whispered to Zoe that it was a good sign.

At last, a boar appeared on the opposite bank. He sniffed the ground, then the air, wagging his tusked head. He was big, probably 300 pounds or more. He entered the water, followed by about twenty more swine. When the herd almost reached the near bank, bedlam broke out. The boars began squealing and thrashing about as dozens of poisoned darts struck. The swine that tried to turn back were cut off by the men in the boats who speared them with bladed blow-guns. The agonizing cries of animals dying and men shouting was deafening as the river turned crimson.

A few of the boars made shore and disappeared in thick bush, with Dai Mai, Zoe, and several others right behind. Men, coming from the village, cut off the boars' retreat, and they suddenly turned back on Zoe's group. It was a dangerous moment. The men readied their spears when they heard them charging back through the jungle.

Total mayhem followed when beasts and men collided. Zoe, as wild as anyone, shouted and slashed with his machete and it wasn't until later, when they were cutting up the carcasses, that he realized how much his legs hurt from being bruised.

They had killed far more than they needed. Dozens of swine floated down the river to be eaten by fish or crocodiles. It was hard work hauling the meat back to the village and it took the rest of the day. A festive atmosphere prevailed, especially since *bali* had sent such fine gifts. Wine was brought out once more and men drank and butchered late into the night. While the fat was melted down and stored in pots, the meat was cut into thin slices and roasted. Other pieces were dried or smoked for later use. Everyone pitched in, except the very young. When they were done, dog-tired and blood-covered, many of the men smiled and spoke to him. Dai Mai said they were grateful for his help.

When he stretched out on his mat that night, his mind kept rehashing the day's events. The Dayaks did everything with relish, whether it was feasting, love-making, working, or killing boars. Zoe had really enjoyed the danger and the excitement of the hunt. How quickly had he been transformed into a knife swinging primate who lustfully enjoyed the gruesome activity. He was sure that a community hunt was exactly what man was designed for, physically and emotionally. While his senses and physical power had been fully tested, he had enjoyed the security of fellow hunters, something seldom experienced in "civilization." It was true community, developed and efficient, where everyone felt involved, and he realized it spoke to a deep need in his own life.

The next day after the veranda was scrubbed down, wine was brought out to begin another day of festivities. Zoe, nursing a hangover, refused the wine and he and Dai Mai sat in the shade of the veranda and watched a blowpipe contest similar to a turkey shoot. The men had tied a rooster by one leg behind a six-inch board. His bright red plumage made an excellent target, but his head never bobbed up twice in the same place.

The shooters were firing in turn at about twenty-five yards and Zoe was impressed with their accuracy. Only the rooster's mobility kept him alive. The weapon was fired from a half crouched position and was absolutely silent—its missile, a nine-inch balsam ended reed. Dai Mai called blowpipes *sumpitans*, which had been painstakingly hand-crafted from six-foot lengths of hardwood.

"Are the darts they are using now poison dipped, Dai Mai?" Zoe asked.

"Oh, no, *tuan*, poison is never used at such times."

Zoe had been impressed with the fast action of the poison on the wild boars. "Tell me, how do you make the poison?"

"There are certain trees in the jungle, the *upas* is one. When the bark is cut, a white liquid comes. It is gathered while still fresh and must come from a healthy tree. It is boiled on a low fire until the liquid becomes very thick and dark. You must taste it to assure the bitterness. The more bitter, the better."

"Did you say taste?"

"Yes, *tuan*. But it will not harm. The poison must enter the bloodstream to kill. Everyone has a favorite mixture which is passed down from father to son. Some comes from the creeper vine, some from snakes' venom. There are many combinations but the effect is the same, to paralyze and kill."

Dai Mai had brought his blowpipe with him in anticipation of the contest. Zoe noticed the mouthpiece had been ornately laminated with metal, that shaft was artistically carved.

"May I see your blowpipe?" he asked. He carefully examined the exquisite weapon. "You must be very proud of this."

"Yes, it was made by my uncle with great care." Would you like to try it, *tuan*?"

"No, no," Zoe said, laughing.

"Yes, you must. Come, it is my turn to shoot."

Zoe, wishing not to offend, followed Dai Mai out to the yard.

Dai Mai shot first and his dart lodged just below where the rooster's head had been. Now it was Zoe's turn. He took a deep breath, blew hard, but the dart fell about twenty feet short.

"I will tell you a secret, *tuan*," Dai Mai said. "When you build the wind in your lungs, keep your tongue over the hole of the pipe. Pull your tongue away quickly, and the dart will go farther."

Zoe tried it, and amazingly, hit the board, though nowhere near the rooster. This brought applause from the other shooters.

Three days later as the festivities began to wane, the chief sent a messenger for him. They sat in the subdued atmosphere of the chief's quarters.

"The chief would like you to know if you still wish to go to Long Bawan," Dai Mai translated.

"Yes, as soon as possible."

Dai Mai and the chief conversed for a moment. "He says he is saddened that you must leave. He would like you to stay."

"Tell him I truly enjoy his hospitality but I must go."

Dai Mai spoke again to the chief. The chief nodded and made an announcement to everyone.

"He says that tonight we will have a final celebration in your honor. In the morning you will leave with guides. We will go by *perahu*, then cross over the mountain."

"You going, too?"

"Yes, *tuan*. I have asked and received permission."

"Great," Zoe said. And Dai Mai smiled broadly.

It was a celebration not soon forgotten. After the first round of food, the Dayaks began drinking in earnest. Since Zoe was the guest of honor, he sat cross-legged on the veranda with Dai Mai and the chief. Small gifts were laid at his feet. The chief gave him a ceremonial bark vest; young maidens, approaching shyly, gave him rattan necklaces or bracelets.

He was impressed when the young girl who had danced that first night, obviously danced once more for him. Her dance was not meant to entice, it was more an expression of sadness that he was leaving. He didn't need Dai Mai to explain it.

He had grown fond of Dai Mai's people. Even though they seldom washed, drank too much, and were hung up on devilish superstition, they had a special quality that greatly appealed to him. That night as he lay on his mat, he had a fleeting thought to stay longer with them—that he had much to learn about their way of life and their communication with the spirit world. Their mystic rituals hinted of secrets to the meaning of life itself, secrets that modern civilization had perhaps overlooked in its mad rush to solve all its problems with hi-tech science.

Maybe someday he would return.

They left at first light and paddled down river, six young Dayaks and a white man clad only in a pair of very ragged khaki shorts and tattered sneakers. They made good time traveling with the current, and the rapids, though swift and dangerous, were skillfully managed.

On the second day they secured the long boat and began the trek to the next river system, since the vessel was too heavy to carry any distance. They cut their own trail through trailing vines and thorny underbrush.

When they arrived two days later at the new tributary, the men set about constructing a new *perahu*. They felled a large tree and cut off a forty-foot length. Using large knives and wedges, they split the trunk in two, then hollowed out one of the halves.

Since the project would take two or three days, pondok shelters from branches were erected to keep out nightly rains. Zoe noticed that each man, upon retiring, went through a little ritual. First, he took a stick and setting it on fire, held it toward the west and prayed. Dai Mai explained that he was saying, "The sun is setting, I will now sleep." Immediately another stick was set afire. Holding it toward the east, he said, "When the sun rises, I will arise and eat." This was done to satisfy *bali*.

Just before dark, a giant bird, black and foreboding, flew over them, his loud, ominous cry reverberating through the foothills around them.

"*Tuan*, see the great Hornbill?"

"Yes."

"It will rain much tonight."

"How do you know?"

"Because of the big bird. It always rains when he makes his presence known. There is a story my people tell of such a bird that appeared in the sky during a tribal feast many years ago. There was a great drought and people were dying. The chief, Matiku, was much loved by his village, and they expected him to do some wonderful thing to put an end to their suffering.

"Matiku ordered a great feast to be held in honor of *bali*, but *bali* was still angry. Death, starvation, and then disease came to the tribe. Human sacrifices were ordered by the chief, but this did not help. One day Matiku announced to his people that he, himself, would be the final sacrifice. His son, greatly saddened, asked to take his father's place. But the chief would not allow it.

"However, the son was so saddened he ran off into the jungle. A short time later a large Hornbill bird appeared flying back and forth over the village, calling out with a human voice, and soon, it began to rain heavily and the drought was ended. The spirit of Mitku's son had taken on the form of the bird to appease *bali*. The boy was never found, and to this day, the ringing call of the bird is always heard before the rains."

"Always?" Zoe asked.

Dai Mai studied him a moment, then smiled. "Well—almost always."

But it did rain that night.

For the next two days progress was slow because they were now going up river again. When they came to the upper highlands, the river narrowed and became turbulent. They abandoned the long boat and picked their way along the river's edge. Sharp rocks brought an end to Zoe's tattered sneakers and soon his feet began to bleed. His knee burned continually.

Up and up they climbed through jagged precipices,

and the jungle changed from dark to pale greens, browns, and grays, muted with mist which blew through the gnarled trees. It was much cooler now at night when they camped on a ridge, which Zoe estimated to be five or six thousand feet above the lowlands.

Toward the end of the ninth day, they reached the crest of the last ridge. They looked down on an immense picturesque valley surrounded by mountains. There were many rice paddies and villages with corrugated tin roofed houses.

"That is the Kerayan Valley," Dai Mai said.

They began their descent.

NINE

It was bright daylight now. Zoe began to cramp up in his hide because he couldn't move freely. Below him on the road he could see agents making their preparations for the 0900 attack. Three more hours to go. He was so close to the compound he could hear bits of conversation from above. Again, he told himself he had no business being so near their perimeter. The more he thought about it, the more convinced he was this operation had been ill conceived. Initiating an action based on the tip of a sole informant wasn't very smart, even if Harding would probably cover up with phony evidence later. Too many had died on both sides.

That the patriots would be so tough was definitely another dropped piece of intelligence. And what about the young zealot hanging on to a cross, evidently merely trying to diffuse a bad situation—it cost him his life. But had he really failed? The whole country had witnessed the government killing an unarmed pacifist. No telling what effect it would have on the millions of fence-sitting joe-six-packs, not quite sure that the continual media hype that all patriots or militia were potential terrorists was really true. He had read some of the patriot literature, and try as he might, he had found little to criticize, except their illogical fanaticism to adhere strictly to an out-of-date Constitution. To him, the whole thing was political, certainly not worth losing lives over. He was weary taking part in a game that made sacrifices on altars fueled by passion for power or bolstered egos.

Maybe it was time for him to make a change, maybe leave the country before it totally fell apart. He had always liked Australia, but lately, it seemed the Aussies were having their problems, too. Somewhere in the world there had to be a place where a man could live relatively comfortably and stress-free. And then, he closed his eyes, and his thoughts drifted to a peaceful time in his life and to a place like none he had ever known before—the Kerayan Valley.

He remembered how he had trekked down the rocky mountain trail with Dai Mai and his men, and had entered the village of Kampungbaru. The setting sun cast long shadows when they wearily made their way to the center of the complex and were surrounded by a hundred young Dayaks, fully clothed, the boys in shirts and slacks, the girls in long brightly painted batik dresses.

"Anybody here speak English?" Zoe asked.

"Yes," a boy with his arms full of books replied.

"Please take us to your chief," Zoe said.

Someone snickered. "I will take you to the headmaster of the school," the boy said and led the way. The young people followed them to one of the small bungalows. When they drew near the house, a pleasant looking, round faced man appeared, smiling.

"Welcome," he said in precise English. "Come in and be comfortable."

They all sat down in straight back chairs in an outer room of the man's house. He introduced himself as Ngir Wusak, the headmaster of the school.

Zoe introduced Dai Mai and the crew and said, "We have come from a village about eight days to the northwest. This is Dai Mai. His people found me after I crashed."

"Are you a pilot?" Ngir asked.

"No. The pilot I was with died in the crash. His name was Jeff Bergman."

"No!" Ngir exclaimed. "Jeff is dead?" His face paled. "How can it be?"

Zoe explained what happened and Ngir sat listening with head bowed, his face twisted in grief. When Zoe finished, no one spoke until a woman appeared who Ngir tearfully introduced as his wife. She was tall for a Dayak and strikingly aristocratic. Dressed in a colorful long dress, she carried a tray of tea which she offered to Zoe, then to each of the boat crew who suddenly looked out of place in their loin cloths. Some of them stared at Sallman's picture of Jesus in the garden hanging on an opposite wall.

"I must get to a radio to send a message," Zoe said, turning to Ngir.

"Yes, the nearest is the government's at Long Bawan. About four hours to the west, but it is a tedious journey." Ngir studied Zoe's cut and battered feet. He ordered water, and when a boy arrived with it, he knelt on the roughly hewn floor before Zoe, and over his objections, tenderly bathed his feet. When he was finished, he left the room and returned with a pair of sandals, khaki shorts, and a shirt that later fit Zoe fine.

"Are there military at Long Bawan?" Zoe asked.

"No, just the district supervisor."

"Maybe we can get a message to Jeff's wife."

"Of course. I will send someone in the morning. Ngir reached for a pad and pencil on a nearby shelf and handed them to Zoe.

"Dear Marcia," Zoe wrote. But he stopped and stared at the pad, seeing a petite cheerleader open his letter and begin to sob when she read his words. After a while he handed the pad back to Ngir. "Would you mind? You've got all the necessary facts."

"Of course."

When it was time for the evening meal, Ngir offered thanks for the food and for Zoe's safe arrival, and Zoe was touched. They ate rice trimmed with chicken and fresh pineapple. They visited some after supper with the village elders and Zoe learned the young people he had met earlier were some of the 200 students attending Bible school there.

They turned in then, the crewmen in a house down the way, and Zoe to a guest room in Ngir's house. Dai Mai and his men would be leaving at first light, and Zoe planned to be up to see them off.

He slept well. It seemed he had just dropped off when a drum began to drone slowly at first, then faster as dogs barked, roosters crowed at the wake-up call. He made his way outdoors in the dark and down to Dai Mai's house, shivering from the chilly mountain air.

Dai Mai and his men were up and eating rice brought to them by Ngir's wife and daughters. Packets of rice in banana leaves had also been prepared for their journey. Zoe sat with them on the mat, accepted a pack, and began to struggle with the words to thank Dai Mai for everything he had done.

"You have been a good friend to me, Dai Mai, a very good friend."

Dai Mai looked down. After a long moment he said, "It has been an honor, *tuan*, to be *your* friend." That's all that was said. When it was time, he shook hands with each of them, but he couldn't resist hugging Dai Mai. Dawn was breaking as they went outside and became aware of singing from a large church on a distant hill—beautiful four-part harmony, rich, full, captivating.

"Who's singing so, *tuan*?" Dai Mai asked.

"Students, I think."

"It is so beautiful, *tuan*."

Zoe agreed. They said a final good-bye, but when Dai Mai turned to leave, he stopped and held out his blowpipe. "Please accept this as a token of my feelings."

Zoe started to refuse but the solemness in Dai Mai's face told him he dared not. There was nothing in the survival kit equal to the blowpipe. Then he remembered his watch. It was an expensive self-winding chronometer, a gift from his mother. She would have to understand.

"Dai Mai, this is for you." He showed him how to use it.

The boy was ecstatic.

They parted then, and Zoe watched the six men trudge up the path that led to the mountain. When they were gone, he put the blowpipe in his room and then sat on a bench on the outer porch and listened to the singing.

All the trials of the past days, the anguish, fear, and pain seemed to diminish as he listened, enraptured. Ngir came out of the house and quietly sat down next to him. A dense mist covering the valley and mountain tops slowly dissipated before the rising sun. Zoe turned to his host. "Beautiful."

"Yes," Ngir agreed, his eyes moist. "Nothing quite matches the sound of a young heart."

"How many people are here in the villages in the valley?"

"Almost ten thousand, mostly Christians."

"Really? How did that happen?"

"In the early thirty's, Christian Alliance Missionaries endured great hardship to come up the rapids to preach the Word to us. When a village became Christian, it would become concerned for a neighboring village and send workers there. So most of the evangelism was done by the people, themselves. But if the missionaries hadn't come in the beginning, I am sure we would still be worshipping idols, practicing witchcraft, in constant dread of spirits and drinking *pangaseth* till we became sterile."

Zoe was reminded of Dai Mai's village. After a moment he asked, "Did your people fight the Japanese during the war?"

"Yes. Especially after the Japanese began killing all foreign missionaries. Our men would catch soldiers in boats coming up a river. They'd fell a big tree, cutting off their retreat, then shoot them with poison darts. They would also hide the missionaries from the Japanese. One, in particular, was a young man named Will-finger. When the Japanese began rounding up all foreigners, he didn't know what to do but flee into the interior with the Dutch. In a letter to another missionary, he said he had prayed and was led to follow a way which was difficult for the body but right for the soul. That if he didn't give himself up, the Dayaks would be forced to lie, and he hadn't come to their country to make them sin. So he surrendered.

"He was kept at Tarakan in solitary confinement. While he was there, an American submarine sank a Japanese ship in the Tarakan harbor and he and a Filipino prisoner were taken out for a vengeful execution. Before he was killed he asked permission to sing, 'Precious is my Lord to Me.' He sang it in Indonesian to the gathered crowd, and when he finished he asked to pray for his captors. They were not willing, and while he prayed, they cut off his head. There were many Muslims and other non-believers watching, and as news of how this man had died spread into the interior, many were converted."

"How did the Bible schools start?"

"Well, through the years we have seen how important it is to train the young people to follow God's ways."

"But who supports you?"

"No one. In 1947, Walter Post, a missionary, told us we must tithe our goats and chickens and rice. He said in that way our church could become independent and strong, for then our pastors and teachers would be supported. So we began. We have learned much about trusting God. But there have been many problems. Christian families are often told to move to the downstream edge of their village, or even completely away.

In one village, a Christian longhouse was burned down and government soldiers had to come. But now there are no more villages in the Kerayan left to evangelize."

"I know of one village outside the valley you might want to put on your list," Zoe smiled, thinking of Dai Mai.

"Yes, I know, I already have made preparations to send two graduates there soon."

"No kidding." Zoe was impressed.

For the next few days he just sat around because of his still tender knee, but when he couldn't sit any longer he would visit a student class, or even attend an evening church service.

One afternoon, a messenger arrived from Long Bawan with a communication from Alliance Missionary headquarters at Jakarta. Apparently, Jeff's wife had taken the news hard but seemed to have rebounded well. She would be leaving for the states shortly. Ngir had asked the organization to dispatch a MAF plane for Zoe, but since the replacement pilot for Jeff wouldn't be arriving for months, someone would have to fly over from Celebes, or some other district, and no date could be promised.

Zoe was nervous about the delay. The longer he tarried, the greater the risk of the government snooping around. He still had the money belt with the phony ID and passport for a cover, but unless his knee improved dramatically, he planned to abort the mission.

Meanwhile, he rather enjoyed being the center of attention with the students. Each day he answered scores of questions from the boys about America. The girls, much too shy, would whisper their questions to the boys. Except for one—Kala. Kala, with her chestnut eyes, raven black hair and tall slender figure would wait patiently until she could ask him a question like, "We hear that in America a young wife must now work to help her husband so they can afford food and shelter. Why is that?" Or, "Children are a gift from God, why is it that America who first sent missionaries to us now kills many babies every year?"

At another time or place he might have blown her off but she was obviously sincere and eager to learn and she made a lot of sense. So he tried to give her honest answers. Gradually, he felt himself drawn to her. He appreciated that she didn't try to market her charms. Always shy and retiring, she had a certain look when she dropped her eyes while talking to him that was starting to give him little shivers. He thought of her often when he lay awake at night.

One warm evening he was sitting on Ngir's porch enjoying the sunset behind the distant mountains, when she strolled past.

"Hello," she said and curtsied.

"Hi," he smiled. "Where you headed?"

"No place."

"Care to sit down?"

She smiled and sat on the edge of the porch, carefully placing her feet on the top stair, and making sure her full length cotton skirt covered her legs.

"So, tell me about yourself," Zoe said.

Even through her flawless bronze complexion Zoe could see the blush. "There is not much to talk about." She sat with legs drawn up under her, her chin resting on her knees.

"Well, how old are you?"

"Sixteen."

Zoe was shocked. He guessed her to be at least nineteen. "Do you like it here, the school, I mean?"

"Oh, yes."

"What's your favorite subject?"

"The Bible."

"Why is that?"

"Because it helps me understand God."

"Okay," Zoe said, going along. "Why is that important?"

"Why?" Kala was amazed. "Because God is the beginning of life, of knowledge, of everything of consequence. You would certainly agree, would you not, Mr. Zoe?"

"Of course," Zoe said quickly.

"You believe the Bible is God's letter to his people, don't you?"

"Ah, yes."

"Have you read it all the way through?"

Zoe was feeling stretched. He had never read one word in the Bible. The only copy he had ever seen was his Mom's big white one, full of dust, on the top shelf in the dining room. "Well, I probably haven't read it as thoroughly as you."

"I like John's Gospel the best. Do you like it?"

"Ah, sure." It was time to change the subject. "There is something maybe you can explain to me."

"What is that?" She cocked her head to one side and smiled at him and he felt a definite rush.

"I was wondering, how is it there are so many Christians concentrated in this valley? I mean, weren't you all headhunters not too long ago?"

Kala burst out laughing, then quickly caught herself

and became serious. "That's true. My father is a chieftain and took many heads when he was young. But not anymore."

"What happened?"

"A young Bible student named Moses came to our village from the island of Alor, near Timor. He told us our idols were wrong for us to pray to, and to prove it, he went into the witch doctor's house, took his idol and burned it, and my father said Moses would die for it. But to our surprise, nothing happened to him. That was the first step for my father. Each night when Moses preached, my father listened very well. My father said he made much sense.

"Moses told us the whole story of creation, the fall of man and the sacrifice of Christ, which the elders understood because our people have practiced blood sacrifice for generations. Moses told us drinking *pangaseth* would destroy us. My father told us he knew it was hurting the people, but he didn't know why until Moses spoke. My father and many of the men were, how do you say it, hooked and didn't know how to break it—but it was demonic, of course."

"Of course."

"On Moses' last night of speaking, my father suddenly sprang to his feet, and like a wild man climbed into the rafters of our longhouse and began throwing down dozens of skulls. It was scary, but funny in a way, because my father was yelling wildly and the skulls came crashing down and people were screaming and trying to get out of the way. But when he came down he was calm and had this beautiful smile, which I just love, because it has never left him. To be sure, a great spirit of heaviness was broken from our house that night.

"The next morning, my father took a long rope and stretched it right down the middle of the village. He called the people out and told them that they must decide who they would worship from that day—the idols or Jesus. Every single person stepped over the rope and our village became a happier place. Before, when the wine flowed during a festival, everyone grew happy, but then, many times in the early hours in the morning, a fight would start, or a young girl would be taken into the forest against her will. I was afraid many times. But when we became Christians all that was changed. So, there you have it."

"Yes," Zoe said, not knowing what else to say.

For a long time neither of them spoke. Zoe thought about some of the unhappy times in his past that were related to alcohol—his buddy in high school who died behind the wheel on a prom date, the many bar fights he had had both in the States and 'Nam—the party in California that nearly cost him his life.

Later that night while he lay on his mat, he kept thinking about Kala and what it was that made her so different from other females he had known. She had a dimension that he could only guess came from her involvement with the spiritual. He suspected she would be one heck of a mate someday to some lucky stud who probably wouldn't deserve her. He even fantasized that he might return later and pursue a relationship. But he knew it was a ridiculous thought. Him, married?

The days wore on and still no word that a plane had been arranged. During that time Zoe became more acquainted with the villagers and realized they knew little of nutrition or efficient gardening. Instead of planting their tiniest potatoes, which always produced stunted crops, Zoe showed them how to plant the "eyes" of a big potato for a much bigger yield. He taught them about planting carrots, cabbage, beans and tomatoes. The beans put valuable nitrogen into the sandy clay soil, badly leeched by an annual rainfall of almost 200 inches and weeds that flourished in the year-round growing season. He explained that they should contain their pigs and chickens and use the manure as fertilizer, not to throw away their rice hulls, but to burn them and use them, as well, to nourish the soil. Dad would be proud he hadn't forgotten the principles of "wise farming."

Those were satisfying and restful days for him. As he learned more about the Kerayan Valley Christians, who called themselves Lundayas, or the people of the upper river, he became increasingly aware they were the happiest people he had ever known. Unlike the peasants in 'Nam, he never saw one long face or one shirker from hard field work. Though he had to admit, they weren't living in the middle of a war, either. But there was always singing and "*puji Tuhans*'" or praise the Lord, throughout the day which was in hard contrast to Dai Mai's people, whose joy was related to how much *pangaseth* they consumed. Even when a tail end of a monsoon blew in one night and washed out most of a new rice crop, no one complained. "God must have something in it," they told each other and just replanted the field.

Finally, almost three weeks after he walked into Kampungbaru, a message arrived that an MAF plane would land about 1:00 the next day. But a request was made as to which direction he would be headed—to his original destination on the Malaysian border or back to Sepinggan.

"Sepinggan," he said, unhesitatingly.

That final evening Zoe sat with Ngir, the teachers, elders, and their families for a special meal given in his honor in the community hall. The women served large platters of rice and pork, papaya for dessert, and afterward, the men moved out to the large front porch and drank tea, which Zoe was really starting to appreciate. Johannes Sakai, an iternant Dayak evangelist, visiting for a few days, joined them.

"So tell us, Johannes," Ngir said to the gray-haired evangelist, "Is God still working mightily among the Punans."

"Yes, He has touched many. Those who scoff have no answer for the miracles, so they are silenced."

"Tell us about the arm, " Ngir urged.

"Yes, in one meeting a man's arm that had been shortened by an injury was lengthened," Johannes answered.

"You mean it grew right out in front of your eyes?" Zoe asked.

"Yes, we all saw it happen."

"That's hard to believe," Zoe said.

"There is a man, Pak Potu," Johannes said to Zoe, "who has witnessed many such miracles. The Lord used him greatly in the *Apo Kayan*. Once he told me about a miracle he experienced with an insane woman, the daughter of a village leader. According to common practice they had put her into a cage. The village was not Christian, but the family called for Potu. All they wanted him to do was pray for the woman, but he said,

'No, we won't do that. The woman's sanity is not as important as you coming to know God.' So they had a Gospel meeting which the whole village attended. He said that while he was preaching, the woman in the cage was listening closely. When he gave them an invitation to accept the Lord several responded, and he noticed a change in the woman.

"They stayed the night and the next morning she was calm. They brought her out of the cage, and Potu said she was almost white from being locked up so long. But from that day on, she was cured, and all of her clan accepted Christ. They were chased out of the village. This happened at *Long Tajau*."

It was late in the evening when the men closed the meeting with prayer. Johannes shared Zoe's room and long after the preacher was asleep, Zoe lay awake on his mat, trying to fit miracles into the theology he had been raised on, which was basically none. His folks were Lutheran, but seldom attended church or discussed religion. He wondered what Dad would think about these testimonies.

At noon the next day, the airstrip at the edge of the village was filled with people. Even the Bible students were allowed to cut classes to see Zoe off. They heard it first, then it appeared over the mountains, a red and white Cessna. The pilot buzzed the field once, checking it out, then started his approach. That little plane was a part of the world Zoe had almost forgotten. Old men and little kids cheered and waved.

When the pilot cut the engine, everyone swarmed to meet him. He stepped down, a young lean guy in new Khakis' and gleaming-white helmet.

"Hi, I'm John Zoe, sure glad to see you." Zoe shook

with him.

"You bet. Jerry Metzger. They sent me over from Irian Jaya to pick you up. These Dayaks sure get excited, don't they?"

"Yeah," Zoe answered. He started to add something, but let it go. They loaded his gifts in the pod under the craft's fuselage. Ngir's wife had given him a colorful table scarf she had crocheted and a rattan sleeping mat. Ngir gave him his personal basket backpack. The elders awarded him a holder and darts for the *sumpitan*, which he still couldn't shoot effectively, and there were smaller gifts from the students. Kala had woven him a red necklace which he now wore.

When everything was loaded, he went around to the passenger side. Ngir was standing with Johannes holding back the crowd. Kala was in the rear with her girlfriends. He wanted to go over to her to say good-bye, maybe even hug her, but he knew his attention would embarrass her. He should have done it earlier. He waved to her and she waved back and he was almost certain she was crying.

Ngir came over and suddenly was hugging him tightly.

"I'll be back," Zoe managed to get out. "Maybe even real soon. Keep that teapot on."

He opened the door and climbed up on the step of the passenger's side. Ngir had his hand raised to quiet the crowd. When it was absolutely silent, Ngir closed his eyes and with his face tilted upward, began to pray aloud.

"Dear Father in heaven. We thank you for Mr. Zoe and the wonderful times we have had with him. May you give him a safe trip back to his loved ones and may he not forget us because we will never forget him. In Jesus' name, amen."

It was very embarrassing, choking up in front of 300 people. But what he felt at that moment, their love, their humility, their sadness at his leaving, was very hard to handle. He climbed in, buckled the harness, closed the door and turned his face away. As the plane taxied to the end of the strip, he saw Ngir and the elders shooing the people safely back. They were fifty feet in the air when they flew past them, and many of the Bible students had their thumbs up—a gesture they had picked up from him whenever he'd pass them in the village.

TEN

He really meant to stay in touch with the Kerayan Valley people and he had written a couple of letters that first year, but as so often happens, the memories dimmed. Kala wrote three times, and though she never touched on it, he knew he never would have stood a chance with her. The man of her future would have to be a man of God, a role for which he hardly qualified.

As he lay in his hide below the compound, her face formed in his mine and he smiled at the memory of her charm and that wit hard to compete with. He wondered what she looked like now.

He truly regretted not returning to Indonesia when he had the strong desire to—to search out what Kala and the others had discovered about life. The years passed, and his own life gradually degenerated to little more than working to eat and waiting to die. He had no wife, the folks were long gone, there was no one who cared if he ever drew another breath. His income allowed him girl-toys and other playthings like his Corvette, Harley and gun collection that helped him get through a crummy existence. But he had no purpose, no cause to champion. He envied the people he waited to kill just above him in the compound—at least they believed in something.

He had never really gotten over his disappointment with the CIA. He would have considered pursuing a career with them as a contract agent, but the Kennedy thing always hung in the shadows, and the way he had been treated when he returned from Indonesia hadn't set well with him. He was told that despite the crash, he shouldn't have aborted the mission since he still had the five thousand, enough to buy another weapon. Never mind his injury, never mind that the Prime Minister would be long gone and back in his own country by the time he got to him. He was debriefed at Fort Bragg and put on temporary hold. And it was during that time he ran into Colonel Dan Marvin in a bar one night in nearby Fayetteville.

The bar was deserted except for a couple of patrons; one, a male hustler in drag, was sitting down at the other end and giving Zoe the come on. Zoe had had three martinis and was about to get up and set the fag straight, when another patron came in.

He sat down a couple of stools away and asked, "'Nam, huh?" He looked at Zoe's ring that the tunnel rats had custom made for themselves in Saigon. The stone was a smooth black onyx with the words, "not worth a rat's ass" and "'Nam" encircling it. The man looked to be in his forties, and Zoe could tell from his face he'd had a few adventures in his life. Some guys you could read like that.

"Yeah," Zoe said, rubbing the smooth stone. "You?"

"Yep. Special Forces, Green Beret. Colonel Dan Marvin." He extended his hand.

"One of those cushy jobs." Zoe smiled and shook with him.

"Right." Marvin grabbed his drink and moved over, and an immediate camaraderie was established that few people who hadn't paid their dues "in country" would understand.

As the evening wore on, it was obvious to Zoe the colonel carried some heavy stuff. It didn't come out until after a few more rounds when his face twisted bitterly as he talked about a friend.

"Hell, we went to school together, dated the same broads, went into Special Forces together, he was the best. Master Sergeant Jerad V. Parmentier. What a waste. Well, it ain't over till the fat lady sings. Right? Some sorry S.O.B. is gonna' pay someday. I don't know how, where or when, but it's gonna' happen." He paused a moment to collect himself. Then he said softly, "I'm pretty sure who the ones in the CIA are."

"CIA?"

"Yep. Certain people were given intelligence and could have stopped the slaughter."

"Sounds heavy duty."

"It is. What happened was, they sent Jerad to Dak to head a company of South Vietnamese mercenaries. As team sergeant, his assignment was to set up an ambush on a Cong company that had been playing havoc in the area. But they got ambushed themselves by a force four times their size. They were all wasted, every last one. A guy I knew who was one of Westmoreland's aids told me later both the CIA and the general's staff received intelligence, but because Westmoreland was miffed that he wasn't in the 'loop', decided to do nothing to save those guys."

"That is pretty hard for me to buy into."

"I know. Me, too, at first."

It was Zoe's turn to buy a round. When his drink was served, Zoe tried it, set it down, and looking around, said quietly, "You know when I was in CIA training at Bragg, they kept referring to the JFK hit as a perfect way to take out a world leader with a four man team. It really gets you to wondering."

"I know. I can't say for sure how involved they were with Kennedy, but I can tell you something that happened to me, personally. In '64 I was training with my outfit, the 6th Special Forces at Bragg, when the CIA showed up and asked for volunteers to attend a special assassin school. Six of us, young and craving action, volunteered. Not long after, my C.O., Colonel Patten, told me to meet a "company" man in an area close to our headquarters. A friend of mine, another Green Beret Captain, met me and we walked to the site and neither of us knew what was up.

"In the shade of some nearby pines, a slender guy, dressed in short sleeves, slacks and sunglasses, flashed his CIA card and took me aside. He wanted to know if I'd terminate a man who was preparing to give state secrets to the enemy. Assuming the 'hit' would be in Southeast Asia I said, 'sure.' After all, that's what I was trained for.

"I asked who the traitor was and was informed he was a Navy officer, a Lieutenant Commander William Bruce Pitzer. He said Pitzer worked at Bethesda Naval Hospital and had to be killed before he retired.

"'No way,' I told him. My understanding was that I

would only be used overseas—I didn't want to put my family through believing I'd deserted when I didn't show up at home. That's how the game was played—take a stateside mission and you disappeared. The agent got really miffed because he'd goofed by telling me the Navy guy's name. He walked over to my friend who was waiting just out of earshot and I headed back to my office. Whether or not he was offered the same mission, I can't say. All I know is, he dropped out of sight and when I tried to trace him years later, there was no record he had even been in the service.

"Now get this, Commander Pitzer was the guy who filmed the original JFK autopsy. He was found dead in October of '66 in his office at Bethesda where the autopsy on Kennedy had been performed three years earlier. Pitzer was shot in the right temple and it was called a suicide, but I and a few others, know better. You know what his great 'crime' against his country was? He had autopsy photographs that showed the entry wound in the right front of Kennedy's head. Somebody in government wanted those photos destroyed, which he refused to do."

"So the CIA took him out."

"Or, at least, engineered it."

"Unbelievable."

"I know. Makes me sick to my stomach. I didn't want to believe it, but I had another thing happen to me when I got over to 'Nam that clinched it for me."

"In May of '65 Prince Sihanouk of Cambodia cut ties with the U.S. and let Hanoi kick Cambodians out of the territory along the border with South Vietnam, establishing sanctuaries on Cambodian soil for the Cong. When I got over there, I volunteered to lead the first covert operation into Cambodia to neutralize the sanctuaries. My command was a Special Forces 'A' team and 792 irregulars from the Hoa Hao Buddhist Sect.

"In June of '66, a CIA guy named McKem flew into my camp in the An-Phu district near the Cambodian border. He told me we were to ambush and kill this Prince Sihanouk 100 miles inside Cambodia and make it look like the work of the North Vietnamese. I took the mission, but on the condition that the CIA would persuade President Johnson to tell the American people about the sanctuaries and officially okay our cross-border pursuit of the enemy. That way we could get medical evacuation, artillery, and close air support. McKem knew, and I knew, that Johnson was allowing our enemy sanctuaries, even against the wishes of South Vietnamese Premier Nguyen Cao Ky. But I was dead serious, hell, we had already buried 200 of our Hoa Haos, wasted by the enemy operating out of those sanctuaries."

Zoe sipped his drink. "I can tell you now the CIA didn't buy it, did they?"

"No. I was too damned naive, I have to admit. I thought I could make it stick. See, I was all they had at the moment and they were a little over the barrel. Five days later, McKem returned to tell me my request had been denied. In response, I aborted the mission and sent the CIA man packing. His last words were, 'You can't fight the system, Captain, you know you can't win.'

"Little did I realize how right he was. Premier Ky began to threaten our irregulars with court martials, and over the next few days, I was repeatedly ordered to bring my 'A' team out of An-Phu. But there was no way I was going to abandon the people we were there to help. They would have been slaughtered. Also, it could have been a ploy to get me out in the open on the river for an ambush.

"I learned a directive went out from the South Vietnamese high command to attack our camp. American advisors with the ARVN regiment were told that I was a renegade Green Beret, leading the Hoa Haos against the Saigon government."

"Nice guys, setting up their own people." Zoe banged his empty glass down hard on the bar.

"You got it. Americans killing Americans—South Vietnamese, same thing. We would have bought the farm. We were getting ready to take on 1500 heavily armed men to prove what, the ultimate power of the 'company'?

"Well, word of all this was sent to General Quang Van Dang who moved immediately to take control of the situation from Premier Ky. General Dang and his senior U.S. advisor, Colonel William Desobry, both flew to An-Phu, and just minutes before the battle, the ARVN regiment was ordered back."

"Close call." Zoe motioned for the bartender.

"Yeah. South Vietnam's President Diem and his brother were finally executed in '63, officially, by order of General Minh—with no loose ends, and no CIA ties to the assassination. But I found out a Colonel Conein of the CIA gave the 'green light' for the coup and you can take that to the bank."

Zoe never saw Marvin again after that evening, but he wouldn't soon forget his words, and when he was eventually offered another assignment by the "company" he turned them down. Years later, in '93, he was watching TV and a PBS special on the Kennedy assassination. Toward the end of the show, 42 names were listed associated with the Kennedy case who had died violently. Among them—William B. Pitzer, the man in charge of the Kennedy autopsy records at Bethesda. He was also to learn from trustworthy sources that Kennedy, shortly before his death, told several people he was going to splinter the CIA into a thousand pieces.

Zoe bummed around aimlessly the next several years. When his dad's health began failing, he did most the farming, but when he absolutely couldn't stand the boredom any longer, he took odd jobs in nearby cities.

One day a neighbor found his dad dead in the barn from a heart attack, and his mom, grief-stricken, died six months later. It was the low point of his life. He grew reclusive, farming the old place just enough to pay the bills. His only outlet was target practice on his range.

And then, one night he watched a TV newscast of an FBI HRT team trying to defuse a hostage situation. The government sniper tried twice to get his man, and Zoe could tell from the shooter's mistakes, someone might possibly need his services. He began writing letters to government agencies. The FBI turned him down flat because he didn't have a degree. What that had to do with the skills he was offering was beyond him. But the reply from the Bureau of Alcohol, Tobacco and Firearms was favorable.

It wasn't the Secret Service, but he would make a

decent living and he was promised plenty of action in his interviews. In short order, he was in Glynco, Georgia, taking an eight week training course that was a snap compared to his CIA training, or even his boot camp in the Army. His first assignment was teaching young trainees the fundamentals of sniper warfare. Borderline boredom, to be sure. However, it wasn't long before he had some serious assignments when the ATF started getting obstentiously aggressive in the war on drugs.

He was cited several times for excellent work in those early years, but he just did his job and minded his own business. From early on, he saw things that didn't set well—manager favoritism, the ever increasing Gestapo tactics that gave the agency a crummy public image, the manipulation of evidence against hard-to-nail gun owners and dealers.

Then came the Weaver case and Waco and Oklahoma City. The rumor was that the agency was somehow involved in the bombing, which he thought was hilarious, until he learned that all ATF and FBI people were told to stay away from the building on April 19. When he saw the film of the little kids being carried out of that building, he splintered the top of his coffee table with a fist.

ELEVEN

A Bradley engine coughed, then came alive—loud, intrusive, as the driver revved the turbo-charged 8-cylinder diesel for the benefit of those in the compound. Zoe looked at his watch. In five minutes the assault would begin. Then the Bradley quieted down and Harding was on his PA, asking the patriots once more to submit to a lawful search. Moments passed, and then, unexpectedly, a bull horn responded from above.

"This is Bob Dunn, Commander of the 'Watchmen' militia. As we've told you people, we will not cooperate because neither the FBI nor the ATF have legal authority to do a search of these premises. The only authority we recognize under the Constitution, and will allow up here, is the County Sheriff."

Harding took a moment to respond. When he spoke again his words sounded measured and Zoe knew he was being careful because what he said would be replayed a thousand times in the media.

"We have forwarded your grounds of refusal to

Washington and are advised by the Attorney General that our search warrant signed by a Federal magistrate is legal and enforceable, so I will ask you once more, will you comply?"

Minutes passed, with no response. The Bradley began moving into position and then, at exactly 0900, over the din of the engine Zoe heard, "Green light, gentlemen," and loud explosions of automatic rifles erupted and the Bradley led the attack force up the access road.

The Bradley was perfect for this type of assault. An M-2 personnel carrier, it carried three crewmen and ten passengers. It had tank-like treads for rough terrain and respectable fire power with two turret mounted guns, an M-242, 25mm chain gun that fired 500 rounds a minute and a 7.62mm coaxial machine gun. The driver used a periscope for protection against sharp shooters.

As ordered, Zoe scanned the two ground level positions with his scope, and soon, both trapdoors snapped open. He saw the rifles appear first, then the faces, and he shot both through the forehead. He rolled back into the gully immediately, crawled to a bush fifteen feet away, and cautiously looked again. Two more shooters appeared and he took them out the same way and again changed positions. When he looked the third time, both doors were down. No doubt they saw they were vulnerable, having lost four personnel so quickly. Now he scanned the windows of the building, but the shooters were firing from farther back in the rooms and he saw no immediate target. He thought about those he had killed. They looked to be very young men, possibly even teenagers. For the first time in many years he felt a queasiness and it surprised him a little.

"Zoe, you read?" His radio asked.

"Zoe here."

"Got a sniper somewhere to the right. He's hit three of our people."

Zoe scanned the entire area with his rifle scope, but saw no one. He grabbed his Kowa spotting scope with its 77mm Fluorite high powered lens and moved it slowly over every possible place a sniper might use for a hide. All he saw were the exhaust gasses of the guns of those firing from inside the building. He doubted if the sniper was with them. He would have to be much higher, maybe in a tree to effectively get to the agents crouched behind the Bradley. And then, amazed at his stupidity, he noticed the grain silo rising above the trees far back on the premises. It was built with concrete blocks, about eighty feet tall, and had no roof.

He moved along the gully another twenty feet for better position and focused the spotting scope on the structure. He started at the top of the trees and slowly made his way upward, block by block. Two-thirds up, he saw two holes where blocks were missing. He went to the very top and studied it a while, but saw nothing unusual, so he went back to the missing blocks.

And then he saw it—the barrel of a rifle, then the scope, and finally, the face. The high magnification of the spotting scope gave him excellent detail and he was startled to see the shooter was a woman. He grabbed the Remington and laid the crosshairs on her face and took a deep breath, let half of it out, and began subconsciously counting—one thousand, two thousand, three thousand—when a realization blazed into his memory.

He put the rifle down and quickly picked up the spotting scope. Eighteen years was an awfully long time. Though he was forgetful of names, faces stayed with him—especially if they were strikingly pretty and vivaciously alive. He watched the sniper get off another shot and disappear once again. He waited. The face reappeared, a pretty woman with ash blond hair spilling out of a camo fatigue cap, the high forehead and those eyes you could never forget, and when the face fully turned his way for an instant, he made positive identification. It was Marcia Bergman.

He sucked in air and pulled back into the gully to collect his thoughts. He remembered that night he had stayed with the pilot and his wife in Borneo. They said they were from southern Illinois and had both qualified for the Nationals as shooters. They had been very upset with conditions in America.

"Zoe, you read?" The radio startled him.

"Zoe here."

"What's going on? We've got another man down."

"Still looking," he said, stalling.

"Johnson, McKee, you found anything?" Harding asked the FBI shooters.

"No sir," one responded.

Zoe lay on his back and looked up at the shoestring clouds in the sky. Though the air was cool he was sweating profusely. The sun, the earth, the war around him drifted away and he slipped into a silent vacuum. His war was within. His mind told him that he had to take her out—she was the enemy killing his people—but something insisted that to kill her would be wrong, terribly wrong.

A few times in his career he had had similar struggles, but he had always managed to shrug them off, to let them get to him would comprise his commitment to his job, to his integrity. He lay the rifle back into position and put the crosshairs on the missing blocks, and once again, began to work on his biofeedback. When the face reappeared in the scope he was ready. He fired.

He thought about it many times, for months after. Perhaps it was the way the FBI shooter, Lon Horiuchi, had needlessly killed the Weaver woman, or it could have been because of the zealot with the cross, or the four youths he had just shot, but at the last instant, he pulled the barrel up and the 168 grain armor piercing round smashed into the wall above her head, exploding several blocks into a white shower of pulverized concrete.

Because of the sniper, the advance had been halted, and during a brief lull in the firing, Zoe's shot rang out, and even as he fully intended to save her life, he signed her death warrant, for his shot and the exploding concrete gave away her position. An order barked over the radio and the Bradley's guns blew the entire top of the silo apart, and Zoe, watching through his scope, saw her body jerk violently when the heavy rounds tore into her.

He turned away from the gruesome scene and hunkered down low in his hide. The advance continued, the Bradley turned its fire power fully on the two story frame farm house of the compound with a vengeance, and it slowly disintegrated.

When the men in black advanced to within twenty yards of the compound and were no longer being fired on, they rushed the buildings. The word came over the radio. The compound was empty.

Zoe collected his things and made his way up the hill. He was in no hurry. For the first time in his career he had compromised an assignment, and now he felt confused, hardly able to think. He knew he would be questioned, for him to miss was unthinkable—everyone knew he never took chance shots. He hadn't a clue what his defense might be. As a matter of pride, he had a thing about lying, and so, if he told the truth, that he couldn't kill her, that indeed, it was starting to get to him, this senseless taking of lives over questionable issues, his career might just end quite suddenly.

When he was almost to the house he veered to the right, to the rear of the property and the silo. He found an entrance in the rear of the structure and had to force open the door because of the debris blocking it. He squeezed through and almost fell over the body of a woman lying face down. He turned the torso over and grimaced at the battered face of Marcia Bergman, her large lifeless eyes staring at him. He turned away in disgust.

He made his way back to the old house that appeared almost unsafe to enter. Both posts supporting the front porch roof had been severed by ordnance and the roof was on the verge of collapsing. He walked into a large front room furnished with old furniture.

The floor was littered with ejected shells. There was total bedlam as agents shouted at one another and tore open cabinet drawers and hammered the walls with their rifle butts looking for hidden contraband.

He walked through the house and out into the backyard and sat down on the stone foundation of an old well. He was thirsty. He looked around for something to draw water. Harding came out of the building.

"Looks like they went underground," he said.

Brilliant deduction. "Yes sir."

"We think we've found a tunnel entrance. I told the men to hold off in case it's wired. Take a look, would you?"

Zoe sat there for a while, then breathing a huge sigh, got to his feet. He made his way past the young men waiting along the walls of the back stairs, their faces betraying their apprehension, to the cellar, and to a heavily timbered door at its far end. With a powerful halogen light someone handed him, he carefully examined the latch and hinges first, then the entire door.

He could be wrong, but his hunch was that the door was not set with explosives, and he wasn't sure why he thought so. He turned to Harding.

"I don't see anything. The door's strong, got to be eight to ten inches thick. Suggest you have your people lay some plastic around the latch and hinges. You won't be able to get anything big enough down here to punch through the door.

"Right," Harding answered and he barked the orders to clear the area.

While Zoe waited upstairs, he thought about the next sequence of events. Harding would ask him to lead them into the tunnel, and once more in his life, he would become a tunnel rat. Old feelings of ice water in his gut started to return. He climbed out of the Ghille suit, borrowed a 9mm HP-5 from one of the men he knew. An hour later he was still waiting. Several applications of explosives were necessary to force open the door. Behind it, the attackers were surprised to find a wall of concrete construction blocks stacked from floor to ceiling and almost six feet in depth.

More explosives were needed to blow a hole through them, and once again, Zoe was summoned. Covering his nose and mouth to protect against the heavy dust, he told the others to wait at the entrance, and aided by the powerful light, picked his way through the broken concrete. The tunnel sloped downward and appeared to be four foot wide and about five feet high. He could have been back in 'Nam. He wasn't surprised to see the tunnel veer off at an angle up ahead. He wondered how they built the concrete wall so quickly then reasoned most of the blocks could have been in place, except for a small opening for the last man to squeeze through and then put the final blocks into position. A very effective way to slow up pursuers.

He reached the spot where the tunnel changed direction and paused. Again he had a hunch he needn't be concerned. Those people weren't the Cong. Still he examined the area carefully for trip wires. Motioning for the others to follow, he began moving more quickly and found several side arteries which proved to dead end into partially dug larger rooms. He estimated he had traveled at least 100 yards in the main tunnel when he came to a three way split, and choosing the middle opening, went another twenty yards and found a ladder and trapdoor above. Throwing the sling of the gun around a shoulder, he quietly climbed to the top and opened the door an inch and listened. He heard nothing. Gingerly, he climbed out and found himself in the dense underbrush of the woods behind the compound that extended down the hill and into a large valley below. He estimated he was at least 50 yards beyond the perimeter the agents had established. Apparently, the "Watchmen" had chosen to fight another day.

Reporting his findings over the radio, he went back to the compound to make a full report, but Harding was nowhere around. He collected his stuff and began walking down the hill when he noticed a large crowd below on the road. He headed toward them. Harding and his lieutenants were being interviewed by the media. Harding was holding up two M-16 automatic rifles and his men were holding several ANFO containers and nitro caps.

"So, what you're saying then is that these ingredients are for making bombs."

"Well, they could be."

"Like Oklahoma City?"

"Not on that large a scale."

"Do you know what they were planning?"

"Based on the tip we originally received, and then finding these illegal weapons and materials in the tunnel would definitely indicate they were up to something."

Zoe walked away. He didn't need to hear any more

bull. He had been the first into the tunnel and he found no ANFO or any other materials for explosives and the weapons looked like the two he had seen for the last couple of days in the front seat of the command vehicle. He went back to his tent and began to pack his gear.

TWELVE

"Charlie Barrows here."

"Charlie, this is Lee Baxter."

"Yes sir?"

"I've just gotten off the phone with Harding over at the FBI. We had a long talk about your man, Zoe."

"Yes sir, is there a problem?"

"Well, there might be. You know I don't have any love for these FBI guys. Harding could have gotten better intelligence before they went after that southern Illinois bunch. Hell, we lost between the two agencies, what, five dead, seven wounded?" He's a small-minded man in a position of power, in my opinion."

"But I thought Washington pushed for this one, it was supposed to be a test case."

"Regardless. The point is, those patriots escaped and nothing was really accomplished, except once again, we all got caught with egg on our face. Even the media, which usually swallows our line, is beginning to question why an ATF shooter took out that unarmed zealot with the cross and the small amount of fertilizer that was found."

"With all due respect, sir, I've felt all along the press should never have been allowed the access they had."

"Well, that directive, I know for sure, came out of Washington. Now the Republicans are screaming their guts out for an investigation that can't help either agency. Harding will no doubt get called, and as ATF regional director, I'll get pulled in, along with you and Zoe—especially Zoe.

"But he was following Harding's orders to shoot on sight."

"I know that. And I told Harding, trying to nail his ass is a little unfair when you consider how his guy Horiuchi took out the Weaver woman who was holding a baby yet, for God's sake."

"Great point, sir, if I may say so."

"Well, its the truth. But there's something else Harding mentioned that I need to verify. He's trying to claim that Zoe blew a fairly easy shot at the sniper.

"I believe it was a woman, sir." They found her laying at the bottom of the silo. But to answer your question, the way it happened was, the sniper shot four of our men and pinned down our advance. Even though Zoe missed, his shot told us where she was and we took her out."

"How old is Zoe."

"I believe forty-five."

"Isn't he a little old for assault work?"

"He's in great shape. Besides, we desperately need his skills, especially in light of last month's meeting. I have only a couple of men who qualify as snipers and if we plan to start using those type of tactics, I'll really need him."

"As an instructor, perhaps."

"Sir?"

"I think we need to get him reassigned immediately, to something low profile. With a little intensive PR, there is a chance we might be able to talk our way out of a hearing. Meantime, put him undercover as a mole somewhere, maybe in one of those militia groups. What about that Johnny Johnson character, the one on short-wave in Houston with the Texas Militia? Zoe would be perfect. It's out of your district and Zoe wouldn't be recognized. He hasn't had his picture in the paper, has he? I mean, he didn't go to that 'Good O Boys' round up and maybe have his picture on that poster 'Media Bypass' magazine printed a year ago?"

"No, not Zoe. He pretty much keeps to himself. Doesn't socialize much."

"Okay. I'll fax what I have on Johnson and alert the Texas office. Have Zoe wear a recorder and pay particular attention to any information that would help build a case for conspiring to overthrow the government.

"And another thing while we're on the subject. I don't want Zoe, or any agent, provoking any illegal activity. That 'plant' Sullivan used in the 'Viper Militia' case was a total idiot. First, he tried to get the group to handout racist literature, then he gives them some explosives and finally he tries to talk them into robbing some banks, all of which they refused to do, though supposedly, they did do some training with the loud stuff. At the hearing, Agent Ott testified their office never told the plant not to push that stuff. As it turned out, there was no hard evidence of any serious crime. All the info they put out and the media lapped up couldn't be backed up at the hearing—even the name, 'Viper Militia' was phony, the 'plant' made it up. Unbelievable. I'll tell you, some people never learn. Some of these districts act like they haven't got a clue what time of day it is, and then they wonder why the NRA runs ads calling us 'jack-booted thugs.'

"Anyway, tell Zoe to study the material carefully so he won't sound like a dummy. I'll send some general stuff on the militia also."

"Should I contact Dees at the Southern Poverty Law Center, or the Anti-defamation people to see what they have on Johnson?"

"You could. Just check out everything they send you because they both have agendas I haven't quite figured out yet."

"I was going to ask you about that. We ran a check on locals around here that Dees had on his list of subversives. They were all respected citizens in their community, and not one of them was in the law enforcement database. When we did on-sight inspections on the Class 3 dealers, everyone of them had proper paper on their automatic weapons and none had explosives."

"I'm not surprised. Dees has his own private war going against anyone who calls himself a patriot or is in a militia. I kinda suspect he plays on the fear of John Q. Public so that he can get donations. I hear his 'Non-Profit' bank account is into seven figures."

"Wasn't he in court recently?"

"Right. His ex-wife accused him of all kinds of garbage. He's no choir boy, to be sure. He's had his hands slapped more than once by the courts for unprofessional behavior, and he's been accused by employees for sexual harassment."

"Doesn't sound like he's a credible source for information."

"Hey, it's not my idea we use him. I don't condone smear tactics, no matter what the cause. What goes around, comes around, and what's happening to our agency these days you might say is coming back around. Just be ready to duck. I intend to keep doing my job and watching my backside. I suggest the same for you. You run a tight district. We get fewer complaints from your district than any of the others. Just stay on top of those gun shows. There's been an increase in parking lot deals, so make sure you have a stake out there. Warn the rookies about entrapment. The ATF has two cases pending and if they go against us right now we'll be a long time getting the funding we need."

"Yes sir."

"Okay. That about covers it. Keep me up to date on everything."

"I certainly will—and sir, I want you to know I appreciate your confidence."

"Well, the older guys like you and me remember the way it used to be; we took a lot of pride in our profession. Sad, things have deteriorated to such a low level. Sometimes I feel dirty no matter how many times I wash."

THIRTEEN

Zoe sat in a coffee shop just off campus at Texas A&M University in College Station, Texas, and studied the file on the local militia Barrows had handed him with his new assignment. That morning he had registered for some fall courses in agriculture under the name of Roy Brewer. Many farmers took courses in high-tech agriculture so it was a good cover. The campus was a little over an hour's drive from Houston.

His new assignment hurt his pride a little. He had worked long and hard to become the best, but Barrows had made it tactfully clear how much management respected his achievements. And it did make sense to go undercover until the clamor about the shooting of the zealot subsided. Barrows never made much over the blown shot on the sniper, and for that, Zoe was grateful. So, for now, he would become a mole, a despicable job in the eyes of some, but he would take the job seriously, and if the truth be known, he did feel a lot less pressure.

The following Wednesday evening, dressed in well worn Levi's, T-shirt and cowboy boots that hid a miniature recorder, he drove his '86 Ford pickup to Houston. The address turned out to be an old Baptist church in the suburbs. He noticed quite a few anti-government bumper stickers in the parking lot.

He entered an upstairs room crowded with people busy socializing. White-haired couples sat next to long haired youth and most everyone carried notebooks. Trying to be inconspicuous, he found an empty folding chair in a back corner, just as everyone quieted down and three men dressed in camo-fatigues entered and sat down behind the podium.

"Greetings," the shortest of the three announced. "My name is Captain Albright. Welcome to the North Gulf Region's Harris County Alpha Unit militia of the Republic of Texas. With me tonight is our regional commander, Ray Caldwell, and Lieutenant Colonel, Johnny Johnson, who has information for us about the Federal Reserve. Please join me in prayer. Dear Heavenly Father, thank you for bringing our brothers and sisters together this evening. We trust you'll watch over us that truth may prevail, that we may be able to enlighten those who are in the dark and that they in turn may teach others in our nation while there is still time. In your Name we pray, amen."

Amens sounded around the room. After leading everyone in the Pledge of Allegiance, he said, "I want to thank you all for taking the time to meet with your fellow patriots. We have several new faces here tonight and we especially welcome any Federal, State, County or local enforcement officers or agents, and we ask at this time that you identify yourself by raising your hand."

One or two looked around the room, but not in Zoe's direction. "Okay, continuing on, I will now read our statement of purpose. Our purpose is to exercise our right under the authority of the Constitution to assemble as an unorganized militia, to support our local elected law enforcement officials in fulfilling their oath to uphold the Constitution, to educate the public concerning their rights under the Constitutions of Texas and the United States of America, and to act in defense of the Constitution, our families, and fellow citizens against all enemies, both foreign and domestic.

"To further elaborate, our founding fathers made a very clear distinction between a militia, which is all the people, and a standing army, such as a National Guard unit. The militia is made up of essentially all of the people in a community between 17 and 45 years old.

"Our country's founding fathers declared the militia as essential to the security of a free state. Today, we find that we have the need to form militias once again. The limits placed on our government by the Constitution have been stretched well beyond the imaginations of our founding fathers. Our right to own firearms is under continued threat. Many fail to see that if the people can't defend their rights, the words of the Constitution are of little use. As George Washington put it, 'Firearms stand next in importance to the Constitution itself. They are the American peoples' teeth and keystone under independence.' An unarmed populous cannot remain free for long.

"The Texas militia is a defensive and disaster response unit. We will fervently defend our families, fellow citizens, and our rights defined by the Constitutions of the United States of America and the State of Texas. We endorse no particular political party, recognizing that as an individual choice. We welcome patriots of all races, for we all are Americans, regardless of our roots. We are nondenominational, recognizing that our country was founded on the principle of freedom of religion, but we strive to ensure that all citizens regardless of race, color, religion, sex, physical characteristics, or national origin have the right and opportunity to due process, including the right to trial by a jury of their peers in a court of law.

"And now, I would like to turn the meeting over to Lt. Colonel Johnny Johnson."

Johnson took the podium, appearing to be in his late '40's, about six feet, and had a very serious air about him. "Thank you," he said. "Before I get into the Federal Reserve, let me explain why I joined the militia. Back in '93, a friend asked me if I wanted to drive over to the siege at Waco to check out what was happening. We couldn't get very close, of course, but we did spend some time in the restaurants and I overheard quite a few comments from the locals like, 'well, we got rid of the idiots' and as I watched the compound burn on TV, I kept asking myself, 'maybe the adults were idiots, but how could the government be so stupid and cruel as to let all those little kids burn to death."

"A year later I returned to take part in a memorial at

the site and spoke with several surviving Davidians, and I came away knowing that, somehow, I had to get involved. Tragedies like Waco should never have happened.

"Now, there's a situation here in Texas that has the potential of another Waco. A group of Texas patriots have done some research and have determined that Texas never legally joined the United States, that indeed, we have always been an independent Republic. We, in the militia, are supportive, but not in the forefront of the fight because we believe the citizens of Texas must decide for themselves by voting whether or not they want to continue under the authority of the Federal government.

"The media, as usual, has ignored this fight, or has portrayed the patriots as idiots. They told you that these patriots have applied for Texas to be accepted into the United Nations as an independent nation. That is untrue. What they did do was serve notice on the World Court that Texas was an independent Republic.

"Arrest warrants have been issued for these patriots and astronomical fines levied. But let me repeat, all these people desire is that this matter be brought before Texas citizens for a vote. If this is denied by the courts, they will not back down, and the militia will stand with them one hundred percent."

Loud shouts of agreement erupted from the audience, several rose to their feet and raised their fists in the air. "Long live the Republic of Texas," and "Remember Waco" they cheered repeatedly.

When it was finally quiet once again, Johnson said with a slight smile, "Now that I have your attention, let me show you why so many people in this country distrust the Federal government and do not wish to be under its authority.

"A real major cause for the many problems in America is the Federal Reserve System. The first thing we must understand is that the Federal Reserve is not a government agency. It is a group of thirteen major banks who control member banks in their districts.

"When our Founding Fathers wrote the Constitution, they specifically stated in Article 1: 'Congress shall have the Power to Coin Money and Regulate the Value Thereof.' Their intent was that power not be put in the hands of private bankers who could charge enormous amounts of interest, and who could actually then control the country by controlling the money.

"For several years after the Constitution was signed, the bankers tried all kinds of tricks to get control. Finally, in 1913, on Christmas Eve, Congress, with many of its members on vacation, passed the Federal Reserve Act, which officially took the power to create money away from the Congress, and gave it to private bankers.

"The 'Fed' began to print Federal Reserve notes, which are still accepted today as money. But we have to understand that these notes cannot be considered constitutional money because Congress ignored the Constitution in passing this Act.

"Some might ask: 'What does it matter if Congress or private bankers create the money? It is accepted by the people as a medium of exchange with which to perform business transactions.' Fine. But what most people do not realize is that this is debt-money, because interest is charged on every dollar created. Let's say that the Federal Government needs $1 billion to finance a project. Since Congress has given away its authority to create money, the government must go to the Federal Reserve. The bankers are willing to deliver $1 billion in money or credit to the government—plus interest, of course. The Congress then authorizes the Treasury Department to print $1 billion in U.S. bonds, in exchange for the loan.

"It costs the Federal Reserve about $1,000 to print the $1 billion. And what are the results? The $1 billion in government bills is paid, but the government has now indebted the people to the bankers for $1 billion, plus interest.

"Thousands upon thousands of such transactions have taken place since 1913, so that now, the government is indebted to the bankers for five trillion dollars, on which the people pay over $400 billion a year in interest alone, with no hope of ever paying off the principal.

"And, to top that, on this $1 billion that the Federal Reserve received in bonds from this transaction, it is legally allowed to create another $15 billion in new credit to lend to states, municipalities, businesses, and individuals. Added to the original $1 billion, they now have $16 billion of credit to give out in loans with their only cost being the $1,000 they spent for printing the original $1 billion lent to the Government. Is it diabolical? You bet it is!

"The bankers create money out of nothing, simply by writing numbers in their ledger books, giving interest laden loans to the American people, allowing them to write checks on their accounts. Using this process, most banks are legally allowed to lend out up to 50 times of what they have on deposit, creating the money out of nothing and then charging interest on it. You have to admit it's quite a racket.

"The United States has plunged itself terribly into debt since the Federal Reserve Act was passed. In 1910, before its passage, the federal debt was only $1 billion, or $12.40 per citizen. State and local debts were practically non-existent. By 1920, after only six years of Federal Reserve shenanigans, the federal debt had jumped to $24 billion, or $228 per person.

"By 1981, the federal debt passed $1 trillion. State and local debts were more than the federal, and with business and personal debts, the total was over $6 trillion, three times the value of all land and buildings in America. Now in 1997, the federal debt has reached the five trillion mark, and it is continuing to grow wildly out of control.

"We could sign over to the bankers all of America, and we would still owe them almost three more Americas. And the debt continues to snowball. Americans have no idea they have been conquered. They have become tenants and debt-slaves to the bankers. Our children and future generations will be paying the debt forever. We are coming to a point where, eventually, the Government will own nothing, the people will own nothing, and the bankers will own everything!

"Back in the 1700's, Thomas Jefferson warned the American people about such a thing happening. He said: 'If the American people ever allow private banks to control the issue of their money, the banks and corporations will grow to deprive the people of their property, until their children will wake up homeless on the continent their fathers conquered.'

"It is conquest through the most gigantic fraud and swindle in the history of mankind. And to think that the key to their power and wealth is simply their legal right to create money out of nothing and to lend it out at interest. If they had not been allowed to do that, they could never have gained secret control of the nation.

"Many are saying we are headed for a depression. Does this have anything to do with the Federal Reserve? You bet it does. Back in the 1930's, when some of you probably experienced what they called 'The Great Depression,' America had skilled and willing workers, good farmland, a highly efficient transportation system, industries, all that was needed to form a rich nation—all except an adequate supply of money to carry on trade and commerce.

"There were other factors involved, but one of the biggest cause of the depression was that the bankers purposely withheld $8 billion from going into circulation by refusing loans to the population, while at the same time, demanding payment on existing loans, so that money was rapidly taken out of circulation and not replaced.

"Because of this control of money, America was put into deep trouble. Jobs were waiting to be done, goods were available to be bought, but there was no money. Food was thrown into the ocean while people were starving. Twenty-five percent of the workers were laid off. The greedy bankers took possession of hundreds of thousands of farms, homes, and business properties.

"Believe it or not, some of the economic experts of that time blamed the moon for bringing about all the economic hardship. Others blamed the politicians. Still others blamed consumers for not spending their money wisely. But the truth is, the depression was caused mostly by the bankers.

"To end the depression, our government borrowed huge sums from the banks for World War II military equipment, which put new funds into circulation. People were hired back to work, industries began to blossom, farmers sold their produce, and the economy boomed.

"The same bankers, who in the early 30's had no loans for peacetime houses, or food and clothing, suddenly had unlimited billions to lend the Government for war purposes. The nation, which a few years earlier could hardly feed its own people, was now producing bombs to send free to the allies. Upsetting? It is to me!

"Just before he died, President Woodrow Wilson is reported to have stated to friends that he had been deceived and had betrayed his country. He was referring to the Federal Reserve Act passed during his presidency.

"We know the bankers, the hidden controllers of the countries, purposely instigate wars, finance both sides of the same war, to frighten the people into going billions of dollars into debt for national defense. They have financed Communism, and then turned around and had foreign aid sent to stop the Communism that they financed.

"The tens of thousands of young people who are killed, and the hundreds of thousands who are crippled and morally corrupted from war, mean nothing to them. In fact, it doesn't even matter who wins or loses the war, as long as all the countries involved are in debt to them. Many of our politicians have become agents of the bankers, while our two political parties have become their servants. No matter who you elect into high office, Rockefeller and his agents will be running the government behind the scenes—you can be sure of it. How else could something so diabolical as the Federal Reserve, something so destructive to the national interest of the people, be allowed to continue so long? They accomplished it by controlling all of the news media and information centers, by controlling the purse strings—to prevent the people from learning the truth. They blame the people for causing the increase in debt and the inflation of prices, when they know that the real cause is the debt-money system, itself. How many of you know that the United States has been in a state of bankruptcy since 1933?"

A few people in the room raised their hands.

"Well, it is a sad fact, ladies and gentlemen, that in 1933, Franklin D. Roosevelt, under the 'War Powers' Act, committed high-treason against every American by signing the Emergency Banking Act which declared the country bankrupt and insolvent, placing the Federal Government into the hands of the bankers as receivers. And that meant that Common Law juries of the Constitution could be replaced with Homage and Advisory juries; the courts would become Admiralty courts which is why judges refuse to listen to a patriot who bases his defense on the Constitution. What this means is that the United States is really governed by the Secretary of Treasury, who is also governor of the International Monetary Fund.

"The IRS, FBI, CIA, ATF, and other agencies, report to that office, as do all U.S. military forces, state governors, etc. Janet Reno gets her check from the International Monetary Fund. The IRS is nothing more than a private collection agency for the Federal Reserve. They put on their letterheads, 'Department of Treasury' wanting people to think they're the Treasury Department of the U.S. when they're the Treasury Department of the Federal Reserve."

Someone gasped in disbelief.

"But wait, there's more," Johnson continued. "Those close to President Kennedy say that he was getting ready to repeal the Emergency Banking Act and reinstate the gold and silver standard, which would solve this nation's indebtedness. With the same stroke of a pen, he was also going to become the second president, after Andrew Jackson, to destroy the credit check book money debt system and put the bankers and compromised public officials up on charges of high crimes under the Law of Nations. On June 4, 1963, he signed Executive Order 11110 to print U.S. dollars with no debt or interest attached, bypassing the Federal Reserve. Five months later he was assassinated. Immediately, upon his death, the printing ceased and the currency was withdrawn.

"Does anyone have any questions about what we've covered so far?" Johnson asked the audience.

For a moment it was very quiet. Then an attractive brunette in a Texas A&M jacket asked, "Isn't there anything we can do, as citizens, to make America healthy again?"

Johnson slowly shook his head. "The only slim chance we have is to put pressure on the government to repeal the Federal Reserve Act of 1913 and demand that Congress again be allowed to create and control the money of the nation.

"With a reform in the money system, private bankers could not rob the people. Government banks, under the control of the peoples' representatives, would issue and control all money and credit. A $60,000 loan made to build a house would require only $60,000 in repayment, with a minor fee, not $255,931.00, as it is now. Everyone who supplied materials and labor to build the house would get paid just as they are today, but the bankers would not get $195,931.00 in usury.

"A debt-free America would mean that mothers would not have to work, but could remain home with their children. Juvenile delinquency would decrease rapidly. The elimination of the usury and debt would be the equivalent of a 50% rise in the purchasing power of every worker. The bankers would no longer be able to steal billions of dollars from the people every year in interest. America would become the envy of the world, being prosperous and powerful beyond the wildest dreams of its citizens.

"Anything is possible with prayer backed up with action. Write editorials in your local newspapers. Write to your congressmen and get others to write.

Even if nothing changes, at least you'll have a clear conscience that you at least tried.

"I have to tell you, though, the cards are stacked against us. Corruption in congress is rampant. We know because of the laws they have passed. Look at NAFTA and GATT. Even Dole admitted phone calls and letters to his office from the public were nine to one against, but he and most other Washington lapdogs of the New World Order cabal voted for these agreements, much to the hurt of America. I have learned that very few in our congress even read these documents."

"You mentioned Rockefeller," a middle aged man, wearing a U.S. Postal Service uniform, said, "can you tell us who some of the other bankers are?"

"Well, the international players include the Rothschild family in Europe, the Lazares Brothers Bank of Paris, Israel Moses Seif Bank of Italy, the Warburg Bank of Hamburg, and in the States, the Lehman Brothers Bank, the Goldman Sachs Bank, Kuhn Loeb Bank and of course, the Rockefeller Chase Manhattan, all based in New York.

"And with that, ladies and gentlemen, if there are no more questions we'll take a break. When we come back we'll talk about the Illuminati."

Johnson left the podium and most everyone got to their feet to stretch. More than a few hit the parking lot to light up. Zoe stood and tried to get some circulation into his legs. He exchanged niceties with the big guy in front of him and was relieved to learn that this was his first meeting, too. Then he headed outside to look for the cutie in the Texas A&M jacket who had gone out earlier.

He found her outside, leaning against a car, smoking. He walked toward her, stretching.

"Man, that is a lot to take in," he said.

"Tell me about it," she said, smiling. She had to be in her early twenties and even through the bulky jacket he could tell every brick was in the right place. With her jet black hair and dark eyes he figured she had to be Italian. He learned her name was Ollie.

"So what's an Illuminati," he asked.

"You just getting started?" she asked.

"You could say that."

"Johnny will do a better job explaining that than I ever could. I'll leave it to him."

"He seems to know a lot of stuff."

"You bet. He started to do some serious digging after Waco. He's really dedicated to spreading the word. I'm thinking of doing my thesis on the movement, but if I do, I'll probably get a low grade. My Prof is ultra liberal and wouldn't appreciate any of this."

"What's your major?"

"Teaching really interests me but I can't stomach the OBE thing."

"What's that?"

"Outcome Based Education. Basically, the goal is to make our kids 'global citizens,' without absolutes, moral values, or religion—with no allegiance to family or nation. Talk about behavioral modification—drives me totally nuts. Psychological testing weeds out the ones who don't fill the bill, like those from very religious or patriotic families, but on the other hand, when it comes down to testing for real academic skills, everyone gets a passing grade, no one fails. Talk about dumbing down a society? This is another United Nations brainstorm that some committee of mental midgets in American education thought was cool. They call it 'Goals 2000', but according to Johnny, the dummies don't know its a carbon copy of Russian education for the past forty years."

"Well, the Russians haven't done too bad. They put a man in space before we did."

"Don't kid yourself. The German scientists they grabbed after the Second World War did that for them. Other military hi-tech, the KGB either bought or stole from Western countries."

Zoe wasn't sure of his ground. She could be totally right, for all he knew. He changed the subject.

"Let me ask you this. Why is everyone here so uptight?"

"What do you mean?"

"When they stood and cheered and all, when Johnson talked about taking a stand."

"Where have *you* been? Aren't you totally freaked out about what the Feds did at the Weavers' or at Waco? You pay taxes?

"Sure."

"You like working almost half a year just to pay off the State and Fed?"

"Of course not."

"You hunt?"

"Yeah."

"Okay. You like Clinton's trying to take your guns away? You probably have no idea, since you're new at this, that those New World Order creeps plan to use U.N. troops to disarm America as soon as we go into martial law."

"Martial law?"

"You got it. Under the National Emergency Act, which Clinton has kept alive through executive order, he can put the whole country under martial law through the stroke of a pen. FEMA takes over at that point and they confiscate guns. But they got a surprise or two coming. The patriots will be in their face."

"You mean people will actually fight the government? They wouldn't stand a chance."

"You think not? There's a conservative 70 million gun owners in this country."

Zoe shook his head. "I don't know, Johnson sounds scary, all this stuff about overthrowing the government."

"What? No way," she laughed. "He'd be the last person in the world to push for that. The whole patriot movement is strictly defensive. You protect your family or your property because under the Constitution you have a perfect right to do so."

"Against whom?"

"Against whom? Don't you listen to short-wave, or get the Internet? Reports are coming through all the time about abuses of federal agencies. Johnny claims there are, at least, over a million political prisoners in federal jails as we speak—anti-abortionists, tax protesters, pastors who refused to allow the government to dictate the curriculum of their schools."

"Laws have to be complied with for the good of the majority," Zoe said, "even though a few people here and there have to be squeezed a little."

Ollie straightened up, took a drag on her cigarette, then ground it into the pavement. "I think you need to do your homework. I can tell you a story about someone who got *squeezed* by the ATF that I personally know about."

"The ATF?"

"That's right. Happened just this year. Changed my whole world. That's how I started coming here, matter of fact. I had an uncle who lived in Russellville, Arkansas—Bill Mueller. When I was a kid I spent a lot of time with his family. His daughter, Sarah, and I were really tight. My aunt Nancy could outcook my mom, especially her pies." She paused, obviously holding back emotion.

"Anyway, Uncle Bill was very outspoken, sometimes I wish my dad were more like that. He never swore. He and my aunt were dedicated Christians, but boy, when he got on a crusade—look out! He was ex-special forces and went into the gun business for a living and made the gun show circuit. He would always have some patriotic literature on his tables, you know, bumper stickers like 'We have the best Congress money can buy'—stuff like that.

"Dad said Uncle Bill told him that after the Oklahoma City bombing, ATF agents approached gun show promoters and told them to quit displaying any written materials, cassettes or videos that were not gun-related. The promoters said, 'No way', but the ATF threatened them until they gave in. This upset Uncle Bill because he believed it was his Constitutional right to display and offer patriotic and Christian materials, so he kept doing it. He told my dad he had sent a written formal complaint to the head of the ATF concerning the illegal strong arming of the gun show organizers.

"Well, the Muellers' got home from a gun show one night and found their place ransacked. Only gun-related items and a few coins were taken. The loss was about $40,000. There were no leads and no suspects. Soon after, Uncle Bill was told by an ex-military man that his name was on a secret 'observation' list at the Pentagon. They found out that several others named on the list had been killed, and their guns stolen. Naturally, my uncle was concerned—he'd call Dad and they'd talk a long time. But he refused to compromise." Ollie paused, and looked out across the street to the farmland beyond.

"In January of this year, their friends found the Muellers' house door open and their Jeep Cherokee and luggage trailer, which they kept loaded with all their gun show wares, gone. Nothing was stolen from the house, no overturned furniture or signs of a struggle. Three weeks later, their vehicle and trailer were found several miles away, empty of the guns and their savings. Aunt Nancy's purse, containing her credit cards, was found in the vehicle.

"In the spring, their bodies were discovered when a fisherman snagged one of them in 20 feet of water in the Illinois Bayou River. All three had plastic bags over their heads, held with duct tape. My aunt and uncle Bill had handcuffs on their legs and wrists. The bodies were discovered 27 miles from where the vehicles were. More than a few people down there believe, without any doubt, that the family was murdered by professionals."

"And you think the ATF did it?"

"Most people who knew Uncle Bill believe that. One guy I know worked for the Pentagon for years told me it could have even been 'lend lease' foreigners who are operating from the 'Special Ops' section, whatever that is." They used Uncle Bill as an example to the gun culture."

"That's a big leap in logic, if you ask me."

"Well, like I said, you need to do some investigating—don't take anybody's word. Uncle Bill's death is not an isolated case. What's your answer for Waco? Were those little kids treated as hostages? No, they were gassed. How long were they gassed before they burned to death? Six hours. Has the government signed an agreement not to use this gas on foreign enemies? You bet. Does the manufacture of this gas warn against its use in enclosed areas? Absolutely. Does the manufacturer of this gas warn that it may cause fires? Yes. Did Janet Reno authorize the use of this gas in an enclosed wooden structure, knowing there were two pregnant women and children inside? Yes, again. So you tell me—why isn't Janet Reno in jail?

"As for the ATF, what's your answer for Oklahoma City? Are you aware some ATF guys have admitted they were ordered not to show at the building that morning, and that not one ATF or FBI guy lost his life in the bombing?"

"So you think the ATF caused that, too?"

"Someone from the government did because some

demolition experts have evidence that drums of fielmenated mercury were attached to the columns. They say, it is impossible that fertilizer and fuel oil in a truck parked outside could have done that much damage. So someone had inside access."

Zoe didn't answer immediately. He knew he'd better watch himself. He had already said too much. Besides, how could he answer her? Oklahoma City had been a big question for him, too. Someone in authority was playing cover up. He had heard about the Mueller case. Some of the districts were getting a reputation for being heavy-handed with Class 3 dealers, but to stoop to murder? And an entire family? It made his flesh crawl thinking about it.

"Man, this is a lot to take in," he said.

It was time to go back to the meeting. He lingered a moment to reach into his boot and push the reverse switch on the recorder. Earlier, he had felt the faint click that the first side had ended.

"First off, ladies and gentlemen," Johnson began, when everyone was seated, "The Illuminati at the very, very top consist of a small group of men, an inner circle of perhaps as few as a dozen or so individuals, who believe they are the 'Lords of Wisdom,' the Illumined Ones. In their minds, they are superior mentally, spiritually, and believe they are the mystical guardians of a holy secret of royal bloodlines and supernatural birthright. This birthright has been passed down through the families through the centuries that have amassed untold wealth. This gives them the ability to dole out rewards to their puppets, whether they be heads of state, the media, politicians, corporate overlords, or religious leaders. This also gives them the power to punish those who cross them. People like John Kennedy, or Robert Maxwell, the publishing tycoon, who became rebels and didn't tow the mark, are simply murdered. The 'inner circle' has no conscience, they are involved in occult practices, and worship Lucifer as their 'Father of Light.' Their wonderful sounding motto 'Ordo Ab Chao' means 'creating order out of chaos.' They may truly believe they are 'seekers of light' but they have been deceived—they are on a one-way path to self-destruction and hell.

"Manly P. Hall, a 33rd degree Mason, in his book, 'Lectures of Ancient Philosophy', wrote that the Illuminati are Masons, but hastens to add the rank and file of the Lodge is ignorant that a very elite invisible society in their midst is dedicated to absolving governments and nationalism, private property and family life, as we know it. They would replace the family with communal education of children. Remember it *Takes a Village* by Hillary Clinton? Surprise, surprise.

"And now, ladies and gentlemen, I'd like to read you something from Texe Marrs' book, *Circle of Intrigue*.

> "'President Wilson's inability to convince the U.S. Senate to go along with his plot for World Government under the guise of the fledgling and preliminary League of Nations, was his downfall. For years he had been under harrowing stress and pressure to fulfill the Illuminist agenda. In 1913, he and congressional puppets of Rockefeller and Rothschild had steered through an unwitting U.S.

Congress the monumentally deceptive Federal Reserve Act, establishing dictatorial control by the Illuminati of America's entire money and banking system.

"'The same year, 1913, Wilson and co-conspirators in the House of Representatives lied and perjured themselves by declaring that the Sixteenth Amendment to the U.S. Constitution had successfully passed through two-thirds of the state legislatures. The Sixteenth Amendment unlawfully crammed the income tax down the workers' throats and was the catalyst for today's Gestapo tactics of Big Brother's Internal Revenue Service. In fact, only a handful of state legislatures had approved the Sixteenth Amendment, not the two-thirds needed for ratification. But the confiscatory policy of the IRS was a major goal of the Illuminati's 'Inner Circle,' and a little thing like 'truth' was not allowed to interfere with their schemes.

"'In 1917, President Wilson and his Illuminist handlers engineered the sinking of the ship, *Lusitania,* in the Atlantic, inflaming the U.S. public and causing Congress to declare war on Germany. Through this bogus conflict, the Illuminati hoped to establish the League of Nations as the embryo for the World Government of the beast to come. But when Wilson failed abominably in 1919, and a stubborn U.S. refused to implement the 'Versailles Treaty' and have the U.S.A. join the organization, suddenly, the President's usefulness to the 'Inner Circle' was over.

"'Within months, it was announced that Wilson had suffered a 'paralytic stroke.' Mostly lying in bed, weak and incapacitated, others ran the affairs of the presidency in his name until his term of office expired. Later, to satisfy the public's questioning of just who had been in charge in the White House, the cooperative media erroneously spread stories that Wilson's wife, Edith, was running things during the chief executive's debilitating 'illness.' Insiders knew better.

"'Together, this Euro-American coalition of conspirators used what they called 'Round Table' groups to found such heinous criminal establishments as the Federal Reserve Board, the Council on Foreign Relations, and in Great Britain, the Royal Institute of International Affairs, that nation's equivalent of America's Council on Foreign Relations.

"'In fact, the Illuminati are keen advocates of organizations. Over the years they have set up literally thousands of frontal groups. Some are sham organizations, operating in name only. Others, like the World Federalists, World Goodwill, the Trilateral Commission, the Aspen Institute, the Carnegie Institute for International Peace, the Rockefeller Fund, and the Club of Rome exercise considerable power and influence.

"'One particularly nefarious and loathsome

Illuminati group is the Order of Skull & Bones, also known as the Skull & Bones Society. In America's *Secret Establishment*, his excellent treatise exposing this 'deathhead corps,' Skull & Bones researcher Anthony Sutton declares:

> 'The Order (of Skull & Bones) has either set up or penetrated just about every significant research, policy, and opinion-making organization in the United States. In addition to the church, business, law, government and politics...persistently and consistently enough to dominate the direction of American society...for a century...'

"'Among the elite alumni of Skull & Bones we find former President George Bush and columnist William F. Buckley, both masquerading as conservatives. We also find such Illuminati bloodlines as the Browns, Harrimans, Dulles, Whitneys, Lords, Paynes, Lovetts, Pillsburys, Bundys, Weyerhausers, Astors, and, of course, the Rockefellers. Their common training ground was Yale University where, not incidentally, both Hillary and Bill Clinton went to law school and were watched over with meticulous and infinite care by their Illuminati handlers.

"'Governmental organizations, set up at the behest of the Illuminati, especially of the international variety, are ever proliferating. In recent decades we have seen the emergence of the United Nations, the International Monetary Fund, the International Labor Organization, the International Bank of Settlements, UNESCO, the World Bank, the European Monetary Institute, and the World Wildlife Fund. Quite recently, the World Trade Organization was founded, with headquarters in Geneva, Switzerland, and a World Environmental Agency is on the way.

"'Through such intelligence and police agencies as the United States' CIA, the Israel's Mossad international spy organization, Britain's MI-5 and MI-6 spook agencies, Europe's Interpol, and the FBI, the Illuminati are busily and greedily extending their Big Brother tactics throughout the globe.

"'...Countless innocent men and women have been assassinated by these governmental agencies, with the CIA, Mossad, and Britain's intelligence agencies being most active in carrying out 'terminations with extreme prejudice.

"'Here are some other examples of contrived crises and created chaos used by the Illuminati to advance their nightmarish scheme for Orwellian World Government:

"'War Invented: On December 7, 1941, the Japanese attacked Pearl Harbor. History now reveals that President Franklin D. Roosevelt, a 33rd degree Mason, and his traitorous colleagues knew in advance that the attack would occur. The War Department had broken the Japanese code. But FDR had committed the U.S. to intervene in World War II and a pretext was needed to cause the American people, very isolationist and anti-war, to willingly back a declaration of war.

"'More war Invented: In August, 1964, President Lyndon B. Johnson claimed that North Vietnamese P-T boats had lobbed artillery shells at a U.S. ship off the coast of Vietnam. LBJ won almost a unanimous vote of Congress as the Gulf of Tonkin Resolution was passed granting the President extraordinary powers to pursue the air and ground war against the Communist foe. Years later, it was discovered that the North Vietnamese had never attacked the U.S. vessel. The incident was a tragic hoax—a contrived crisis.

"'Diseases Invented: In the 1980's, the media began sounding the alarm that a dreaded virus, HIV or AIDS, threatened the lives of tens of millions of Americans. Evidence, however, indicates that the U.S. Army's biological warfare laboratories may well have created the AIDS virus and that the United Nations World Health Organization may have engineered its spread in Africa and elsewhere. The results could have been anticipated: fear, anxiety on the part of the masses, and the empowerment of the homosexual lobby. But an even more ominous consequence may lie in store in coming years if the Inner Circle decides to use viruses to decimate and depopulate the Earth.

"'Environmental Crisis Invented: In 1966, a classified government study, 'The Report From Iron Mountain,' recommended that a global environmental crisis be contrived to engage the masses in a holy war to save Mother Earth. The Illuminati saw that the environmental scare could also be used to further their plan for world government by international treaties like the 'Convention on Biological Diversity.' This would destroy private property rights and enable the creation of a World Environmental Agency which would erode American sovereignty and enforce global law.

"'Corporate overlords tied in to the Illuminati network immediately began pumping millions of dollars into environmental organizations such as the Sierra Club, Greenpeace, the Nature Conservancy, and others, creating today's massive Mother Earth propaganda lobby. By keeping America's vast forests of timber from being harvested and huge reserves of oil from being extracted, the Fascist, corporate overlords of the Illuminati have also artificially kept prices of these natural resources sky-high. The environmental movement is a financial bonanza for the rich.

"'Overpopulation Crisis Invented: Also in the 1960's, the Rockefellers and other Illuminists decreed that a disastrous over-population problem existed, although there was absolutely no scientific evidence whatsoever for this conclusion. Millions of dollars were pumped into organizations such as the National Organization for Women, Planned Parenthood, and Zero Population Growth. Again, draconian bureaucratic measures of control were propagandized as necessary to solve this created crisis, including mass abortions and euthanasia.

"'Healthcare Crisis Invented: In 1992, co-Presidents Bill and Hillary Clinton, acting on behalf of the Rockefellers, declared by fiat the existence of an imaginary healthcare 'crisis.' Their proposed solution was to socialize America's entire healthcare system and bring it under stiff, fascist government control. Fortunately, their attempt failed, but trust me—this scheme will be resurrected. It's too lucrative a scheme to lay fallow for long.

"'The Crime Crisis Invented: Also in 1992, the 'crime problem' became a major focus of the controlled media. Despite FBI statistics which actually showed decreases in serious crimes, the public was fed dramatic 'case' stories by the media about the victims of crime. Always, handguns and the artificial category known as 'assault weapons' were portrayed as the enemies of America. According to the Illuminati-inspired propaganda, violent criminals weren't the problem—just guns. Result: Congress passed the Brady Bill and President Clinton successfully demonized the National Rifle Association and other Second Amendment groups. America is moving fast down the road toward a police state as the BATF, FBI, DEA, IRS, Secret Service, Customs Service, and dozens of other police agencies are targeting owners of guns for harassment and extinction.

"'Terrorist Crisis Invented: In 1993 and 1995, so-called 'terrorist' bombs caused devastation and loss of lives at the World Trade Center in New York City and at the federal building in Oklahoma City. Shocking news reports, covered up by the controlled media but accurately reported by alternative, patriot media, indicate government involvement in both of these horrendous tragedies. Result: The Illuminati conspirators stirred public outrage against patriotic militia and other America First groups and pushed anti-terrorist bills through Congress.

"'Meanwhile, in federal court in New York City, during the trial of the Arabs accused of planting the bomb at the World Trade Center, the prosecution was stunned when the defendants introduced a tape recording which implicated the FBI itself in the monstrous bomb attack. In the tape recording, an FBI infiltrator is overheard offering the Arabs the bomb device and explosive materials. On the witness stand, this same FBI operative admitted that the FBI had provided the explosives and the bomb used by the Islamic plotters, and he confessed that he had been paid the sum of one million dollars to go undercover and deliver the deadly materials to the terrorist.

"'Anti-Semitism Crisis Invented: During the 60's, 70's, and 80's, and on into the 90's, numerous radical groups advocating racial conflict and anti-Semitism were unearthed by the media. The media constantly bombarded us with frightening tales of KKK lunatics, neo-Nazi haters, and so forth. Then, evidence began to leak out that almost without exception, every one of these arcane and violent groups were set up by federal authorities. When such groups were 'outed' and exposed, it was always federal infiltrators and affiliated non-governmental agencies who were responsible.

"'It now can be concluded that, while there are no doubt some haters in every society, the U.S.A. included, the most visible of hate organizations featured so prominently in the newspapers and on TV news programs are government founded and funded. Result: The Illuminati has been incredibly successful in getting the public to accept outlandish gun control laws, hate and thought-crime investigatory agencies.

"'A Gestapo police state has been created in America, complete with the awesome

> powers to tap phones, break down doors, terrorize the citizenry, plant or destroy evidence, confiscate property, and even to murder innocent victims—all in the name of justice. It is plain to see that modern history provides account after account of the Illuminati and its agents interfering in the affairs of men and nations.'"

Johnson closed his papers and looked out into the faces of the people. His eyes traveled around the room slowly, looking at each person as if trying to communicate with their very souls. Then he looked at Zoe, and what Zoe read he didn't quite understand. Normally, Zoe could stare down anyone, anytime, but not this time, not in this place. He felt a hot twinge in the back of his neck and he turned away and looked at the wall.

A discussion followed and became louder as people desperately sought answers for what they should be doing individually to help the country. Zoe tried to stay focused, to learn of any discussion to overthrow the government. Just before the meeting closed, a young guy dressed in camo-fatigues stood up and asked loudly, "all I want to know is, where do we draw the line?"

No one answered him.

FOURTEEN

Zoe had mixed emotions when he pulled out of Houston three months later. He was glad to be going back to Illinois and to his farm, but he would miss campus life and the student friends he had made. He saw Ollie at two other militia meetings in Houston, then she dropped out of sight. He sent in his reports and tapes to Barrows immediately after each meeting. Barrow's last letter was short—"wrap it up."

He arrived at the farm before dark on Friday and spent the weekend cutting firewood and mending fences. Monday morning he drove to St. Louis, anticipating his next assignment. Since he hadn't heard anything more about a congressional inquiry, it was possible things had cooled to the point he'd be able to get back into action. Making his way to Barrow's office in the rear of the government building, he was told by the secretary to go right in.

"How are you, John?" Barrows said, smiling. He arose from his desk, and stuck out a hand. He looked tired. He was less than two years from retirement. Zoe would miss him—he was a good manager and he didn't b.s. his men.

"Well, it was a nice vacation," Zoe said, sitting down. "And a real experience."

"I bet. I gather it wasn't what you expected."

"That's putting it mildly."

"I've gone over the tapes and studied your notes. I doubt if the government could make a case."

"Well, that's what I thought. Their whole philosophy is defensive."

"There might be something to this offer of their's to go to any state to help another patriot 'under attack', as they put it. Crossing state lines to assist in an armed resistance would definitely make a case."

"But they have to do it first," Zoe said.

"Right." Barrows sorted through papers on his desk. "There was one statement Johnson made that I put aside. Here it is, 'our objective is to throw down the New World Order and to re-establish Constitutional law, the Republic, the Bill of Rights, and to make sure the Declaration of Independence is ours—that is our objective.' The question becomes, to what extent is he willing to go?"

"He's dedicated. But he is definitely not a terrorist. Wanting the country to return to the way it was long ago under the Constitution only makes him a little weird, but that's all."

"I know." Barrows studied the papers. "I see you questioned the statements made by the coed about the Mueller case."

"Yes, I wanted to ask you about that. Her conclusion sounded bazaar."

"And you also questioned the Oklahoma bombing statements she made."

"Well, at first I thought she was off the wall, but the more I think about it, a few things don't add up."

"Like what?"

"For one thing, why were our guys told to steer clear of the building that morning? And how is it we just happened to have a bomb squad in the area, witnesses reported seeing before the bombing? This isn't the first time I've heard stuff about this—some of the guys have been discussing it. It sure looks like someone had prior knowledge. That bothers me big time because a lot of people got sacrificed. For what, I ask myself? What idiot would sacrifice all those people because of some cause? According to Johnson, we have a shadow government working for the New World Order crowd that's using the agencies to disarm the people in order to completely control them. "What's going on? Who do I work for, anyway?" Zoe knew he was getting a little heavy handed with his superior, but this thing had been festering inside him.

Barrows slouched down, his fingers pressed to his temples while he studied Zoe intently. After some time he began to speak very softly, looking out at the secretary in the outer room. She was far beyond hearing range.

"John, there's a lot going on I'm not privy to. This agency has changed drastically in the past three years. But because you're one of the few people still around that I feel I can trust, I'll tell you what I've learned—how much is gospel, well, only time will tell.

"Supposedly there are elements in our agency, the

FBI, Secret Service, maybe all the services, who indeed have an agenda. My information is that this element, I've heard it called 'The Order of One', got McVeigh and his friends to blow the building and helped him with the explosives and other details." It was supposed to be a sting operation, but I'm not buying. McVeigh doesn't strike me as a mass murderer—he's an idealist with some scruples. Could be he only intended to blow an empty building but got there late. But then he could see the place was milling with people. I could be wrong, but I feel he was lied to, maybe he was just supposed to deliver the truck, I don't know."

"But why take the building down in the first place?"

"Supposedly, this element wants the public soured on the patriots. They chose April 19th, one year after Waco, then used the media to try to blame the militia groups, like the one in Michigan, except they couldn't make it stick.

By the way, I have it on good authority that, according to ex-CIA chief, Colby, Clinton wanted Waco as example for the Bosnians, that the same could happen to them if they didn't settle their differences.

"I also learned that two CIA guys, Black and Jackson, are suppose to have sworn affidavits by two Justice Department officials that they were part of a committee of ten who planned the bombing. These two justice department guys stated that the bomb was supposed to go off at 6:00 a.m., with no one around, as a scare tactic to get anti-terriorism bills passed and funds for our agency and the FBI.

"Also, get this. Supposedly, a Secret Service agent

overheard shrouded talk in the White House regarding the bombing the day before it happened. He didn't understand the significance until the details of the blast and the President's propaganda speeches that followed started matching up with what he'd overheard."

"This stuff if very hard to believe."

"Hey, I'm not selling. I'm merely telling you what I've been told. You and I have already discussed the hit on JFK. How far up the ladder do you think that went? And what about the World Trade Center?"

"What about it?"

"The FBI could have stopped it."

"How?"

"By calling it off. Or by building its bomb with harmless powder. One of the FBI conspirators, a former Egyptian army officer, secretly taped his meetings with his FBI handlers. This guy, Emad Ali Salem, said the FBI had planned on building the bomb with phony powder and grabbing the people entrapped in the plot. But the informer, who is heard lecturing his FBI handlers on the tapes, said real powder was used and his people didn't do it.'

"The FBI crowed about its investigative prowess after its remarkably swift nabbing of the suspects, based on debris found in the bomb's crater. The truth is, the FBI knew the suspects all along, and gave them the bomb."

"But why, for God's sake?"

"I'm telling you, this element has an agenda—they're trying to speed up anti-gun legislation. Look how fast the anti-terrorist bill got ram rodded through Congress after Oklahoma. And the funding came through, didn't it? Now the FBI's quietly setting up a new heavily armed division which will take over whenever a lethal confrontation occurs in the country.

"Pending an O.K. from the White House, this task force and the Pentagon will move swiftly to deal with the patriotic groups. Right now, they're waiting passage of legislation that will erode the Posse Comitatus Act sufficiently to allow them to use the military against civilians. Some of the military brass I know are dead against it. They fear that when the militia leaders are taken, there will be considerable violence leading to suspension of various civil rights under martial law."

"They're probably right. The people at Johnson's were not bashful about picking up arms against the government if they felt threatened."

"I know. There's a real push to learn where all these people are. For the past 18 months, Socom, the Pentagon's Special Operations Command, has had a special section at the JFK center gathering intelligence, and from what I gather, it covers a wide spectrum—probably got their guidelines from Janet Reno. Besides patriots or militia groups, it includes anyone who defends the Bible, believes in Christ's second coming, goes to weekly Bible studies, home schools, stores food, and God knows what else.

"Socom estimates there are about one million Americans affiliated with militias, or other patriotic groups, about 100,000 of whom are considered violent, and seriously expect an inevitable confrontation with the government.

"Their plan of action, which they refer to as 'decapitating the militias,' is to move suddenly against militia leaders and instructors, taking them from their homes at night; particularly, all former military 'Special Ops' people who have been instructing the militia throughout the country."

"How is it so many different people got suckered into going along with this program?"

"Money. A lot of big bucks have been handed out, some of it in the form of government grants, most of it in bribes, or bonuses."

"Banker money, like Johnny Johnson says?"

"If you buy the New World Order concept, probably so. For a long time I thought all this conspiracy talk was nuts, but the more I listened to your tapes, the more things began to make sense. There's a real push around here to get the older guys into early retirement. I understand the brass in the military were told to get in line with the New World Order, or take a hike. They've been retiring in droves.

"Also, every government enforcement agency is gearing up for something big to happen. I've been ordered to send my more promising young guys to Ranger school, to accelerate our sniper program and fine-tune dynamic entry. Every other memo I get is about house to house search, or how to secure an entire neighborhood. They never mention drugs. They're definitely going after the guns."

"What about the people in enforcement who won't go along?"

"Oh, they'll go along or get pushed out of the way. And don't forget that nice bonus they'll be promised. But if I figure this right, as soon as they're no longer needed, they'll be replaced with FinCEN because they can't be trusted. After all, if they betrayed the oath they took once, they'll probably do it again."

"How does FinCEN fit in with the MJTF?"

"The Multi-Jurisdictional Task Force was put together by Bush as a national police force and consists of National Guard, local police and street gangs. FinCEN is more of a secret police."

"Did you say street gangs?"

"You got it. They call it the 'New Frontier.' In Chicago in '93, they got 200 gang leaders from 28 cities to agree to accept training, funding, and get this, they've been promised on the QT that when they make a house entry they can keep anything they seize, even if its only merely crime related—cash, guns, stereos, and, hey, there's always the women in the household to be had. So you see, whereas guys like you and me might hesitate, these guys will barge into any situation because they're highly motivated. But when they're terminated, then FinCEN takes over. FinCEN stands for Financial Crimes Enforcement Network. They're heavy into computer tracking of financial crimes like money laundering and can reach anywhere on the globe. Supposedly, they're using mercenaries from Germany, Holland, Belgium, France and even Gurkas from Asia."

"Gurkas?"

"Right. Out of Nepal, part of the 3500 Hong Kong police outlined in the '93 Brady Crime Bill. Ski masks are effective in covering their identity. Our military can't be trusted to fire on U.S. citizens over gun seizure, so we've shipped them overseas for police action there—all under United Nations charter agreements signed by our Presidents. We probably have 300,000 foreigners over here right now, all training in urban warfare."

"300,000? You got to be kidding."

"I can even give you most of their locations. Fort Polk, Louisiana, of course, is a U.N. training center. Forty different countries have gone through there in recent years. Then there's Fort Lewis in Washington, Fort Benning in Georgia, Fort Drum in Montana—restricted areas in north and south California, central Texas, the eastern seaboard, Cincinnati, you want more?"

Zoe was amazed.

"If we get into martial law we'll all be out there picking up guns. FinCEN will pick up the resistors, relocate them to FEMA detention camps. They'll use heavy lift aircraft like Chanooks because ground travel will probably not be dependable. First stop for the dissidents is the processing centers—Oklahoma City west of the Mississippi, and Fort Drum east of it. From there they'll be flown to 23 major detention camps and twenty minor ones for permanent placement or elimination. A lot of military bases that were supposedly closed have been converted into holding sites, easily spotted by new barb wire always facing inward to keep people in."

"Are those the FinCEN guys flying those black helicopters?"

"A lot of them. It wouldn't surprise me if it wasn't FinCEN that took out the Mueller family. I've spoken to Jenkins, ATF manager in Arkansas. I know him pretty well, and he says he's positive none of his people were involved, but he's just like me, out of the loop, so how sure can he be?"

Zoe stood up and walked over to the window and looked down to the street. It was noon and a nice day, and the street was filled with office workers at hotdog stands, or sitting on park benches, eating their bagged meals. In the distance he could see a river boat pushing a whole string of barges up the Mississippi.

He stood there a few moments, then turned to Barrows. "You know, that first night that I listened to Johnson talk about the Federal Reserve and the Illuminati I thought he was totally nuts. This is America, the great invincible, untouchable super power. But now it looks like we're about to self destruct. How did it happen?"

Barrows cleared this throat. "I'd say greed is the common denominator. But who do you blame most, politicians who sell favors, or citizens who cheat when they can get away with it? It's like a cancer, it spreads when the good people of the country get careless and only care about full bellies and the good life and don't want to get *involved*. I think it was Göethe who said, 'Let everyone sweep in front of his own door, and the whole world will be clean. But somewhere along the line, a lot of good people in this country decided to let George do it."

Zoe sighed. "What I don't understand, is how people in enforcement can trash the oath they took."

"The kids we're hiring now were never taught the Constitution, or hardly any morals, for that matter."

Zoe shook his head, disgusted. "Well, I've been

itching to get back into action, but if I'm supposed to shoot some farmer because he won't hand over his heirloom, I'm sorry, I didn't join this agency for that kind of work."

"We don't have to cross that bridge, yet. As for your next reassignment, Baxter's on leave, someone's sick in his family. Since it was his directive, we'll have to wait until he returns. Meantime, how about doing some training for me? Maybe check out some gun dealers, take these young bloods with you."

"Sure," Zoe said, "why not?" He took a step toward the door and stopped. "I pity the people who have to go after the guns in Texas." And then he walked out.

FIFTEEN

"Okay, let's see if I forgot anything," Doug was saying as he looked over his notebook, "auto-sears for converting automatics, tubing and fender washers for silencers, altered serial numbers, anything else?"

"There's more," Zoe said. "Just remember, having tubing or washers isn't illegal, but it might mean he's fooling around. Your real item is his paperwork. Always go over it with a fine tooth comb—every gun has to show."

"Gotcha. By the way, thanks for asking for me. I promise to stay on my toes."

They were headed east out of Champaign, Illinois, in Zoe's pickup to check out a gun dealer in Danville, and two in Indiana. Zoe saw Doug's name on the trainee list, and even though he talked a lot, Zoe had decided the night they were together at Marion the kid would do what he was told, keeping hassles to a minimum.

"Some of the guys from Chicago were saying their

manager told them there's an agenda to put all major manufacturers and dealers out of business real soon," Doug said, lighting this sixth cigarette in the last half hour. "Supposedly these people are the hardest to fight in court because they've got bucks and hire classy lawyers. The idea is to drain them dry with legal fees till they're bankrupt and plead guilty to a lesser charge, and still end up in prison."

"We get any more gun laws passed, we'll need the entire U.S. army to enforce them," Zoe said. "Just be very careful about entrapment, don't do something stupid like offering to pay under the table for an illegal item, okay?"

"Gotcha. These guys from Chicago, they're something else. They've got a sting operation against dealers down to a fine art."

"Yeah?"

"Yeah, the way they explained it, the agent takes an SKS or a Mack 90 into a dealer that's been worked on to fire full auto, but very clean, so nothing shows. He makes up a story that he could use some cash, so the dealer offers him, say, $75 for an SKS. He shows up just before closing time, so the dealer doesn't have a chance to play with the piece.

"Next morning, second agent saunters into the store, browses through a lot of guns and finally settles on the SKS. Now if the guy has a firing range in back, so much the better. The agent buys the piece, tries it out on the range, and bingo, he has his man on felony charges for sellin' an automatic. Cool, huh?"

"I guess."

"But wait," Doug said excitedly, "here's the good

part. The agent tells the guy, 'You know, you're looking at a felony charge here of $10,000 in fines, and ten years in prison. Now, with a little cooperation on your part, I can get this substantially reduced.' What choice does the guy have? He agrees to give up his inventory and pay the fine, but if he can come up with anything on other dealers, he stays out of prison. Of course, he loses his licenses, so he's out of business, which was the objective in the first place. Those Chicago guys got it made. They're all driving big cars with the percentages they get."

"They told you they get a piece of the action?"

"No. But I could read between the lines, they made some hints."

"Ever occur to you that they were pulling your chain?" Zoe checked his map. "We're coming into Danville pretty soon. I'll drop you off at a restaurant and visit this guy alone. Two of us going in is too obvious. I want to poke around, he may be hooked into the militia."

He dropped Doug three doors away from a restaurant to be less obvious, then pulled into a gas station, and after gassing up, asked to see a local map. White Tail Gun Shop was on the edge of town.

He found the old store front building and climbed out of the truck, dressed in Levi's, boots, baseball cap and a light leather jacket. His 9mm Glock was holstered inside his waistband at the small of his back.

The first thing he noticed inside when he opened the door was a big yellow flag on the wall behind the counter with the words, "Don't tread on me" under a coiled snake. A beefy older guy with gray beard and close set eyes stood behind the counter. It was chilly for September and a pot belly stove was going in the corner, surrounded by three men in bib overalls. The air was heavy with smoke. The place appeared to be more of a general store than a gun shop.

"Hi," Zoe said to them, smiling. "Getting a bit nippy." He walked to the glass counter that encased a large selection of automatics and revolvers. "Been thinking of buying a gun," he said to the dealer, and he walked slowly along the counter, examining the firearms, "something for self-protection, what would you recommend?" The men around the stove were watching him.

"Well, how large you want to go?" the dealer asked. "The bigger calibers have more stopping power, but are heavier to handle and cost more to shoot. You can buy a thousand rounds of 9mm for a hundred dollars, .45 ammo is currently two hundred."

"Really?" Zoe said, acting surprised. He took a glance behind the counter at a desk piled high with stacks of paper and various gun paraphernalia. He didn't see anything illegal, but judging from the mess, he wondered if the guy's paper was in order. "I don't know beans about them, what would you recommend? Maybe something in a small automatic?"

The complaint on the guy was that he and his cronies occasionally set off explosives in the field behind the store. That was not illegal, but after Oklahoma City, anyone even remotely connected to explosives was to be investigated as a possible terrorist. Zoe wondered about the flag.

"Okay, look at the bottom shelf," the dealer said.

"You've got a choice of an HK, a Beretta, a couple of Springfields—"

Zoe squatted down and pointed to a weapon. "Let me look at that shiny one there." And, too late, he realized that the maneuver probably caused his jacket to ride up and reveal the partially hidden Glock in his waistband to the three men behind. He was right. When he stood up, the dealer was pointing a .357 magnum at his chest.

"Put your hands on the counter, easy like. Charlie get the gun."

"What's the problem?" Zoe demanded.

"Why don't you tell us?"

"I just came in here to buy a gun."

"Mister, you've been eye-ballin' this place ever since you walked in. You act dumb, but you're packin' a concealed weapon and that's not legal in this state. What's your game?"

Zoe sighed. "I'm an ATF agent, just doing my job."

The dealer studied him for a moment. The three men, all over six feet, hovered menacingly over him, one of them was examining his gun.

"Maybe, maybe not. You could have been checking us out for a holdup, too."

"That's nonsense."

"Where's your I.D.?"

"Back pocket." Zoe moved his right hand slowly to his hip pocket and took out his wallet. He started to flip it open, but the dealer reached over the counter and grabbed it. He studied it for a moment. "Looks like it might be all right, but then again, it ain't too hard these days to have cards like this made up."

"That's nuts. Call my office in St. Louis for verification. The number's on my business card, there on the other side."

"That's long distance."

"I'll pay for it."

Keeping the .357 trained on Zoe's chest, the dealer reached for a phone and punched out the number. "Busy," he said, and tried it again.

Zoe recalled the agency's two lines were constantly overloaded during business hours in recent months. They were due for updating when funding came through. "That line is busy a lot," he said. "Why don't you call your local police chief."

"Don't have one. Last one died of a heart attack and the city hasn't made a decision on the new man yet."

"Call the County Sheriff."

"Can't do that, either. He's in Florida on vacation."

"Who else has any authority we can reach?"

"You're lookin' at him. I'm the Chief Deputy Sheriff."

Zoe tried to think. He couldn't believe he had allowed himself to be compromised. He thought about trying to reach Doug at the restaurant, but didn't want to embarrass himself in front of the kid. He hoped a line would open up soon. "You might put the gun down, I'm not going anywhere."

The dealer laid the magnum on the shelf behind him and tried the phone again. The line was still busy. "Looks like we'll just have to wait," the dealer said, and he pulled out a cigar and lit up, making sure Zoe got his share of the smoke. His eyes began to water.

"Mind if I relax?" Zoe asked, starting to straighten

up.

"Relax all you want, but keep your hands on the counter."

Zoe returned to his position and the dealer continued to study him and puff on his cigar.

"You say you're with the ATF. Why would anyone want to work for a scummy outfit like that?"

Zoe felt himself flush. He was getting irritated with this jerk. "It's not that bad a job. It's got good benefits, and all."

"I can't think of a more despised government agency, except maybe the IRS, of course.

"Why do you say that?" Zoe asked, a little too defensively.

"Why? I'll tell you why. For years, the ATF has set up innocent folks with phony evidence, used blank search warrants to bust down their doors, then lie against them in court and bankrupt them through heavy legal fees.

"They went after Koresh at Waco on a bogus charge and tried to cover their ass on a phony child abuse case and 17 little kids got burned to death. They set up a pacifist in Idaho on a shortened shotgun charge and when he wouldn't rat on his neighbors, their FBI cronies shot his wife in the head while she was holding a real lethal weapon, a 10-month old baby. That was after they shot his boy in the back, of course."

"What about that kid with the cross over by Marion?" one of the others asked.

"That's right," the dealer agreed. "That was another example of the ATF acting like the Gestapo, trying to do an illegal entry without any real justification. So this kid, Scott White, holds up a cross to try and defuse the situation only to get his head blown off. People around here thought the kid threw his life away for nothing, but I don't think so. I think when it got shown on the 6 o'clock news across the country, a lot of people realized, for the first time, what their government was capable of, even those airheads who thought the government was right at Waco were shocked. People around here are still talking about that kid."

He paused for Zoe's reaction who had become tight-lipped and was staring down at the counter.

"Ever hear of Lou Katona from Ohio?"

Of course Zoe had. His office had discussed it for weeks. In 1992, ATF agents raided Katona's house and made the largest firearm seizure ever from an individual—worth over $100,000. The raid was based on alleged forged gun registrations, but Katona was later cleared by a grand jury.

"I've heard of him. So what?"

"I know his dad pretty well. One heck of a gunsmith. After the ATF raided the son, he decided to take them to court for damages, so to get even, they had his dad under indictment for sixteen months on some phony charge. It's crap like that that's got so many people PO'd in this country. Did you know the younger Katona's wife had a miscarriage as a direct result of that raid?"

That Zoe didn't know. He wondered how he would have felt in Lou Katona's shoes. The one major regret he had about never marrying was that he didn't have a son to raise, to take hunting, to teach how to shoot, to share things with.

While they were talking, Charlie had taken the phone and was continually trying to reach St. Louis. Finally he said, "I got through. Who do I ask for?"

"Ask for a Mr. Barrows," Zoe answered.

The dealer took the phone and soon was in a heated discussion. After getting a careful physical description of Zoe, the dealer ended the conversation with, "just do me a favor, Mr. Barrows, you send any more agents into this county, you have them check in at the Sheriff's office, okay? They don't have to come sneaking around, asking stupid questions, taking us for dumb hicks, like this fellow did. Thank you and goodbye." He slammed the phone down. "Give him his gun, Charlie."

Zoe thought about his next move. He was mad and embarrassed enough to call Barrows and request an immediate raid, but he had no evidence. He was well aware some AFT offices raided dealers on the slightest pretense. But that wasn't the way he did things. "Now that that's settled, I would like to see the records for all your guns," he said.

The dealer groped under the counter and produced a ledger. Thirty minutes later, every gun had been checked, and surprisingly, accounted for. All that was left was a reason for the explosives. Maybe if he could get the guy talking, and luckily, just then, the dealer asked, "Like a cup of coffee?"

He was a little surprised at the offer, but he surmised the dealer might be having second thoughts about having gotten rough with him. "Sure, black will be fine."

He was offered a chair by the stove and they all sat down. And, as he listened to their comments, he realized they were just like his dad, farmers struggling daily to be able to live meagerly, but comfortably, and dream about that new pickup they hoped to buy someday. Their complaints about government intrusion into their lives he had heard before, but when they spoke in detail of their friend having his farm foreclosed, or the effect of NAFTA on their farm prices, he couldn't help feeling a little guilty working for a government that could cause such distress.

In a lull in the conversation he asked, "What's with the flag?"

"Well," said the dealer, "That flag says exactly what a lot of folks around here feel. Don't tread on us. We're mad as hell and we ain't takin' much more of the government's nonsense."

"So what do you intend to do?"

"For starters, we ain't givin' up our guns. We don't care how many tanks the government sends down here."

"You got that right!" Charlie exclaimed. The others agreed.

"So you would actually fight the government."

"That's right."

"Would I be right in assuming you boys are in the militia?"

"That's correct," the dealer said, without hesitating. "And we don't care who knows it. When you go back to your people, all we ask is that you get your facts correct. 'Don't tread on me' means just that. A rattler doesn't ever go on the offensive. But you better not step on him. Under the Constitution, we have an undisputed right to defend our homes and families against any unauthorized force."

"And who determines what an unauthorized force might be, you?"

"No, not me," the dealer answered. "The supreme law of the land, the Constitution. And the second amendment is crystal clear that citizens have the unrestricted right to own firearms."

"Even teen-aged gangs?"

"The gangs' problems are not guns, but lack of love and supervision of a family. That's why these kids join gangs, they're really looking for acceptance. Take all the guns off the street tomorrow and you'd still have murders—by knives. More kids are killed in cars, or for that matter, by drowning each year in this country than by guns, so why don't we outlaw cars and swimming pools? If you ask me, a big problem in this country is the socialist news media that is constantly stirring up the water until the public is totally freaked out, and demands that the government get rid of all guns. And that's just what the New World Order creeps want. Look at history. First they cause a problem like, for instance, the Oklahoma City bombing. Then they accuse anyone who opposes them for the tragedy, just like Clinton did when he blamed everybody who was politically incorrect, even talk shows. Then they offer a solution—pass more anti-terrorist laws that deny more of our rights. When they get our guns, we'll become their slaves"

Zoe cleared his throat. "So you believe there's a conspiracy?"

"You're darn tootin!" The dealer said. The others agreed.

"Who's behind it all?"

"A small group of demon possessed idiots bent on ruling the world through communism, that's who."

"Communism?" Zoe couldn't help but smile. "I thought that threat died with the Berlin Wall coming down."

"Don't kid yourself. The media would have us believe that, but I don't. I've done some digging. I'll bet you didn't know that the Communist Manifesto calls for an income tax and a central bank, just like our Federal Reserve, and that the United Nations was started by a convicted Communist spy by the name of Alger Hiss."

He waited for Zoe to respond. When Zoe didn't, he continued, "you weren't told in school, I'll bet, that Franklin Delano Roosevelt, a hero of Bill Clinton's, in 1933, forced your dad and mine to turn in all their gold. One week after he did that, he raised the price of gold to $35 an ounce, doubling the net worth of the bankers and other elite who were warned to move their assets out of the country. Of course, the media never told the American people they had been ripped off, royally. Doesn't that sound a little like a conspiracy to you?

Zoe didn't answer.

"There was an eyewitness to the Kennedy assassination that wasn't killed by a *freak* accident. He was a friend of mine, who happened to be sitting on the railroad bridge overlooking Dealey Plaza. He saw two men with rifles shoot the President. He kept his mouth shut and lived. All the other witnesses who came forward turned up dead, just like the long list of people associated with Clinton in Arkansas. So why did the Warren Commission and the media hide the truth from the American people?

"Of course, these witnesses are always 'suicides,' like Vince Foster. Maybe the president didn't order those 'suicides.' Maybe he just depressed those 40 or so victims so much, they killed themselves." He paused to take a sip of coffee.

Zoe thought about it. It was very hard for him to accept that the President was guilty of those deaths. He knew if it could be proven true, it would change his life drastically.

"No, Mr. Zoe," the dealer was saying, "there's a conspiracy all right, and a major player is the media, whether they all realize it, or not, they are pawns in the hands of the New World Order crowd.

"The question we all need to ask ourselves is, are we going to keep our God-given rights as spelled out in the Constitution or meekly submit to the New World Order? We ain't got a chance if we don't start fighting. We need to quit looking the other way when we see a corrupt cop, or judge, dump on a little guy who can't fight for himself, or a politician making bad laws. People like you working for the government need to know you're a perfect tool for tyranny, a willing slave, ready to believe the party line, one of the soldiers who will fire on his fellow countrymen for refusing to turn over their guns." He paused, took a long puff on his cigar, and studied Zoe.

Zoe finished off his coffee and stood up. "My dad

would have enjoyed talking to you, he felt the same way you do about some things. But right now, I've got a schedule to keep. There's just one more item—"

"What about you, Mr. Zoe?" the dealer said, getting to his feet. "Do you believe like your dad?"

"Well, he's dead now. But to tell you the truth, I don't know what to believe anymore. I see the country changing fast for the worst, but I have no answers. I just do what I'm told and let other people do the worrying."

The dealer shook hands with him. "By the way, in case you didn't know, that's what the Nazis used as an alibi at the Nuremberg trials."

"That's interesting. Before I leave though, I need to ask you why you are using explosives? We received a complaint."

"I figured that was really why you were here. Well, the way I see it, I've got three options," he paused a moment, scratching his beard. "I can give you a song and dance, I can tell you the truth, or I can tell you its none of your damn business." He smiled broadly.

"Well?"

"I think I'll go for option three. But hear me clearly, we're not looking to harm anyone. Just like that flag says up there, 'don't tread on me.' If the government stays where they belong and quits passing laws that take away our rights, we'll be just like kissing cousins."

Zoe smiled and walked out.

He didn't go into details when he picked up Doug, nor did he talk much during and after they checked out the last two dealers. They overnighted at a motel and drove back to St. Louis in the morning, and all the time, he couldn't shake a sense of frustration.

He took two weeks of the vacation time he had coming and tinkered around the farm, tending to various long neglected repair jobs. Dad would not have approved of his slothful habits. To break up his work, he went out and shot on his range two or three times a week, and was pleasantly surprised to find he hadn't totally stagnated.

Barrows still wasn't sounding hopeful about his returning to his former job, and he wondered if it would ever happen.

He spent evenings cleaning his guns and listening to an old short-wave receiver dad had used for years. All the talk at the meetings in Houston about government abuse reported on short-wave had made him curious. He held a basic belief in a voting system that, for the most part, allowed good men to run the country. But when he heard the short-wave reports of victims who had survived Waco, it confirmed to him that the congressional hearings he had watched on TV had been whitewashed. He remembered his conversation with Ollie, the Houston coed, when he heard General Partin, retired army demolition expert, give a report on short-wave that his detailed examination of the bombed Oklahoma City federal building revealed it had been destroyed by charges put against each column, triggered by the truck bomb. That, when his report was sent to every congressman and senator, not one called for an investigation.

One day, Zoe found a patriot mail order catalog in the file Barrows had given him and he sent away for the books: "Circle of Intrigue" by Texe Marrs, "Cheque Mate" by Jeff Baker, "Like a Pale Horse" by Bill Cooper and "The Mark of the New World Order," by Terry Cook. He found books on the Federal Reserve and the Communist Manifesto at the library, and when he examined the Manifesto, couldn't believe he was reading a synopsis of what he saw happening in America.

1. Abolition of private property.
2. Heavy progressive income tax.
3. Abolition of all rights of inheritance.
4. Confiscation of property of all emigrants and rebels.
5. Central bank.
6. Government control of communications and transportation.
7. Government ownership of factories and agriculture.
8. Government control of labor.
9. Corporate farms, regional planning.
10. Government control of education.

He was astonished to learn from Tom Robinson's book, "Renegade Government—USA" that Title 26, the so-called IRS Code, was not positive law but merely a House Regulation applicable only to the ten square miles around Washington D.C. and the territories of Puerto Rico, Guam, and the Virgin Islands. The IRS had no authority whatever to lien, levy or seize property from citizens not living in those areas. He learned that the IRS also used Title 27, part 70, as its authority to seize assets, but when he read that section, discovered that it specifically referred only to

ATF officers, not the IRS.

He was never an avid reader, but once he started on the subject, he had an insatiable appetite. For the first time in his life, he actually read the Declaration of Independence, the Constitution of the United States, and the Bill of Rights. In fact, he studied them in depth, and when he finished, he more fully understood the dealer in Danville. He ordered the VCR tapes, "America in Peril," by Mark Koernke, and, "America, It's Not Too Late" by Dick Bova and "CIA Mind Control" by Mark Phillips and Cathy O'Brien. There *was* a world of information out there, confirming that Americans had been lied to, swindled, and many, murdered by their own government. He became totally convinced there *was* a conspiracy to turn the U.S. into a third world country, and soon. There was, no doubt, an agenda to take guns away from citizens.

When his vacation ended, he halfheartedly reported to work. Barrows assigned him a desk job, but as he went through the motions of shuffling endless piles of paper, his thoughts kept returning to the patriot books and tapes that cried out for justice. He was tempted to stay in his shell of security, lose himself in his work, and "let George worry about it." But he had read a quote from Cicero of ancient times in Robinson's book that he copied and kept re-reading until he almost memorized it.

> "...there are two kinds of injustice; the positive injustice of the aggressor, and the negative injustice of neglecting to defend those who are wronged. Not to defend the oppressed and shield them from injustice, is

> as great a crime as to desert our parents, friends or country. In neglecting the duty of defending others, men are influenced by various motives. They are reluctant to make enemies; they grudge the trouble and expense; they are deterred by indifference, indolence, and apathy; or they are so fettered by their own pursuits and occupations, as to abandon those whom it is their duty to protect. Some men say they prefer to mind their own business, and think, that in so doing, they wrong no one. They thus, escape the one kind of injustice only to rush into the other."

One morning in early October, Barrows called him into his office.

"John," Barrows began, "I called you in because I'm getting a little concerned. To be blunt about it, you're driving everyone around here nuts."

"Oh?"

"You and I both know you hate getting stuck behind a desk, with a passion, and that's why you've been so uptight."

Zoe looked out the window behind Barrows. He didn't respond.

"Obviously, I can't override Baxter's directive, but I can get you a temporary change of scenery. Are you interested?"

"Doing what?"

"When's the last time you been to church?"

"What?"

"Church," Barrows said, half-smiling. "There's a guy down in Indianapolis, a pastor, who's been a real pain in the butt to the IRS. They called us. Supposedly, he's got some enemies who've been calling the IRS. Lately, the calls are about a militia group that's getting very active in his church. This confirms other reports of greatly increased activity in the area. Management wants us to investigate. Do you think you could go down there and quietly check things out, without getting into trouble, that is?"

Zoe smiled slightly, knowing Barrows was referring to the gun dealer. "Sure. No problem."

SIXTEEN

Sunday evening, October 13th, 1996. Pastor Greg A. Dixon stood in the pulpit of the Indianapolis Baptist Temple and addressed several hundred brethren of his 1,000 member church. He was a short man with graying hair and disarming smile.

In the third to last pew of the church, trying to be as inconspicuous as possible, sat a slim man with receding sandy hair, dressed in leather jacket, jeans and cowboy boots.

The choir had left the loft and the only other person on the platform was an attractive blondish woman about forty, stylishly dressed in a conservative black suit. She wore very little makeup, her only jewelry was a small silver cross around her neck.

"The IRS is controlling the churches and preachers in America today," the pastor began. "Most of you know the IRS has a 3.6 million dollar notice of lien on our property, a totally illegal act, because they did it without a court order. How can they do it? They are the IRS. They are independent, not even an official government agency. They make up the rules as they go, and only use the law when it is expedient.

"We had relinquished our IRS 501(c)(3) tax-exempt status on Dec. 31, 1983, and for the next ten years, were left alone. As of that date, we were no longer sinning against the Lord by acting as a publican in the collection and remitting of withholding taxes from brothers and sisters who ministered at this church.

"Many pastors, in fact, most people thought we were insane, but in our hearts, we knew it was not the function of a New Testament church to collect or remit taxes to the government, nor can a true church be a business by IRS standards. A New Testament church cannot be an agent nor informer for the government, neither can it be required to keep records. There is no law that requires a church to pay withholding taxes, and indeed, income tax is a voluntary tax, and if servants of this church wish to volunteer, it is their business.

"A real problem today is that preachers and Christians don't study the Bible. Most of the time, they just mouth what others say the Scriptures mean. We talk about the autonomy of the church and then turn right around and register the church with the State through incorporation, licensure, registration, etc. Without so much as a whimper, we keep records for the IRS and follow the whims of every little tinhorn bureaucrat that comes along, all in the name of 'rendering unto Caesar.' It would be far better to render unto Christ that which is His.

"My friends, there's no doubt in my mind that there is a concerted effort on the part of this government to use the IRS and other agencies to silence all dissent to the New World Order by muzzling preachers. The prophet, Isaiah, said that the preachers of his day were 'dumb dogs, they cannot bark.' We have the same problem today. A 501(c)(3) church pastor does not dare speak out against corrupt government. He knows what will happen.

"It started with tax exemption back in the 30's. The IRS said to the pastors, 'we have some goodies for you. You can get housing and automobile allowances.' The preachers lined up to drink at the trough, and if one preacher in America cried out against this wickedness, I don't know who it was. I've checked the records. Some of the greatest men of God who ever lived on this earth ran to the trough and sold their souls and the future of the church in America.

"My friends, I'm not jumping on anybody. I participated in it. I did it ignorantly. But I will never again take God's money that people tithe to this church and finance the godless activities of the government.

"I want to share some information with you tonight that came from a former military intelligence officer in the Pentagon. On February 8th, 1994, a confidential memo signed by Janet Reno was sent to United States attorneys in Mississippi, Louisiana, Alabama, Georgia, South Carolina, Idaho and Montana. They were instructed that the FBI would be conducting extensive investigations and surveillance of right-wing, political and fundamentalists religious individuals and organizations in these states. Dossiers on targeted individuals are to be compiled and retained in Washington at the Justice Department. In the event of a widespread uprising, these individuals and organizations will be viewed as potential terrorists. What this boils down to is that outspoken citizens who would preserve the Constitution will appear on Reno's list of subversives.

"Also, I have here an article from the 'New American.' They took it from the military journal, 'Perimeters.' This journal of the Army War College published an article by Major Ralph Peters which identifies American patriots as the next enemy, defined as primitives in a warrior class which must be attacked. Now that's where we are in America today. You ask, what is our hope? My friends, if God does not help us, there is no hope. We're going to have to get serious with Him.

"Now, this next information will astound you. I have here, a list of executive orders that have been signed by the President. Executive orders are not passed by congress, but are an end-run around the Constitution.

"It was through an executive order that F.E.M.A., the Federal Emergency Management Agency was established. The director of F.E.M.A. has the power of absolute rule over U.S. citizens and resources, should martial law be declared by the President. All previous existing laws are suspended.

"Once Americans are brought under this system, United Nations peacekeeping forces will be employed to maintain law and order.

"Here is a list of these orders:

11002-Empowers the Postmaster to register all men, women, and children.

11003-Seizure of all airports and aircraft.

11004-Seizure of all housing and finance authorities, to establish forced re-location of citizens, to designate areas declared 'unsafe' to re-locate entire communities, etc.

11005-Seizure of all railroads, inland waterways and storage facilities, both public and private.

11051-Provides the office of emergency planning complete authorization to put the above orders into effect in times of increased international tension or economic or financial crisis.

10995-Seizure of all communications media in the United States.

10997-Seizure of all electric power, fuels and minerals, both public and private.

10998-Seizure of all food supplies and resources, public and private, and all farm and equipment.

10999-Seizure of all means of transportation, including personal cars, trucks, or vehicles of any kind and total control over all highways, seaports and waterways.

11000-Seizure of all American people for work forces under federal supervision, including the splitting up of families..If the government deems it necessary.

11001-Seizure of all health, welfare and education facilities, public and private."

As Pastor Dixon read his list, cries of disbelief and anger erupted from the audience. When the outbursts subsided, he said, "Already there are hundreds of trailers being prepared with their own power generators, etc., to be used as F.E.M.A. offices that can be setup anywhere across this nation as soon as martial law is declared. They will enforce these executive orders to the letter and bring about the persecution of the Church in America as never before. Church property, equipment, etc. will be seized. Christian children will be taken from their parents to be forcibly re-educated into the doctrines of the New World Order, while the parents are taken to detention camps already established.

"Through F.E.M.A., Christian radio and television stations will be seized and silenced. Famine will be rampant as food supplies are seized and given out only to those who comply with the New World Order mandates. And the mandate? An identification computer chip in your hand or forehead.

"'Oh, you say, I'll never accept that.' Well, my answer to you is, if you haven't the courage now to speak out against evil, what makes you think you'll have the courage later to say 'no,' especially when it means the bank won't take your mortgage payment because you don't have a computer chip?

"Putting a bumper sticker on your car is not enough, my friends. If you don't have the courage to call in to talk shows, give your congressman holy heck, get into the faces of that school board that oversees the contamination of your child's mind—if you're not willing to start doing things like this, then don't call yourself a Christian.

"Some of you here tonight may be using Romans 13

as an excuse for not defending your rights and your childrens' future. Just remember, when Paul wrote his epistle about obeying the government, he was sitting in jail. He had gone to prison on numerous occasions for violating the edicts and laws of the land. Do any of you actually think that if Paul had meant that we were to obey every law, regardless of how it conflicted with God's laws, that he would have violated the very words he wrote? Of course not."

Pastor Dixon paused and searched the faces of the audience. "My question to all of you tonight is, what are you willing to do, starting tomorrow morning, to help stop the soon-to-happen enslavement of you and your children? If you are afraid, ask the Lord's help. Come out of the closet and walk into the bright light of faith, with your head high. As for me, I will never stop, lay down, or give up fighting for freedom and justice and I trust everyone here tonight feels the same."

Pastor Dixon gathered his papers, took a deep breath and said, "And now, brothers and sisters, it is my privilege to introduce our special guest," and he turned and smiled at the woman sitting behind him. "She is a truly remarkable woman of God and champion for the Gulf War veterans. Captain Joyce Riley, please come and tell us what's on your heart this evening."

Joyce Riley reached into a black leather case at her side, and taking out a folder, went to the podium.

"Thank you, Pastor, thank you all for allowing me this privilege of addressing you," she said, smiling warmly.

"I am here tonight because I love my God, I love my country and I love my fellow man. My message to you is not a happy one and I wish it weren't true.

"My story begins in 1991 when I decided to return to the service. In the late 1970's I had served as a flight nurse in the Air Force. I left the military and was living my life when I learned of Desert Storm and that trained flight nurses were needed. I went back to Kelly Air Force Base in San Antonio and volunteered. As it was, I didn't go to Saudi Arabia because of the cease-fire, but I did serve on a C-130 aircraft with a rank of Captain for about six months. After that, I returned to Houston to my job as a heart, lung, kidney and liver transplant nurse. But I became ill and no one seemed able to help me. I began doing research, and with God's help and proper medication, eventually recovered. In the process, I learned some astonishing information.

"Gulf War Illness appears to have come from three major sources—Biologicals and chemicals that Saddam fired at the U.S. and coalition forces via his Scud missiles, inoculations of experimental vaccines and Pyridostigmine Bromide pills forced upon our troops by their commanders, and blowback from destroyed bunkers and factories that contained chemical and biological weapons.

"There were 28 countries in the coalition and 27 of them have come down with GWI. Only France's soldiers do not have it because France did not let its troops take the experimental inoculations and pills. When their troops were exposed to Scud missile attacks, or began to have symptoms, they immediately administered Doxycycline and their troops quickly recovered.

"Our government did virtually nothing to protect our people even though they knew what Saddam would use—since we sold the biological warfare agents to him over the prior five years. When gas masks and chemical protection were used they were found inadequate, not designed to protect against sophisticated germ warfare agents.

"These germs were made in Houston, Texas, Boca Raton, Florida and other laboratories in the states. They were passed through the Centers for Disease Control and through companies such as American Type Culture Collection in Maryland and sold to Saddam Hussein as late as 1989. Our government was involved.

"A staff report, issued in December '94 by the Senate Committee on Veterans Affairs, stated that troops were ordered to discuss their vaccinations with no one, not even with medical professionals needing this information to treat adverse reactions. Why the secrecy? What was being hidden? Of responding veterans who had taken the anthrax vaccine, 85% were told they could not refuse it, and 43% experienced immediate side effects. None of the women given botulism toxoid were told of pregnancy risks.

"Why is the government so big on inoculating everybody? Every newspaper in the country has had a front page picture or article on inoculation. In Houston, you can drive down a certain street where nurses are lined up to inject you as you stop and put an arm out the window. Why? America, we have to stop holding out our arms to anybody that comes along and says, 'we're from the government. We are going to help you. You need this shot.' Not me! I received too many shots during the Gulf War and I paid dearly for it. I will never do that again. Know your rights.

"May I remind you, that this isn't the first time our government has experimented with drugs and chemicals on U.S. citizens. A good example is MK-ULTRA. It involved the experimental use of LSD on the public without their knowledge. The Central Intelligence Agency notified the University of Maryland that the school may have been involved in so-called mind-bending tests and drug experiments sponsored by the agency between 1953 and 1964. The CIA identified where the tests were done, and that they were going to protect all the researchers involved with the program with confidentiality. However, those that were experimented upon do not even know they were involved in a test. These experiments involved 44 colleges, 15 research foundations or chemical companies, 12 hospitals and three prisons.

"Another example I hope you remember, because I believe it is the origin of the AIDS virus. In 1970, House Bill 15090 appropriated $10 million to the Department of Defense to make a synthetic biological agent. It states: 'we believe that within a period of five to seven years, it would be possible to produce a synthetic biological agent that does not naturally exist, and for which no natural immunity could have acquired. Within the next five to ten years, it would probably be possible to make a new effective micro-organism which could be different in certain important aspects from any known disease-causing organism. Most importantly, it might be damaging to the immunological and therapeutic processes upon which we depend to maintain our relative freedom from infectious disease. '

"Basically this says it will destroy a person's immune system. In 1975, five years later, the first recorded 'AIDS related death occurred. The report also states: 'this is a highly controversial issue and there are many who believe such research should not be undertaken, lest it lead to yet another method of mass killing of large populations.'

"A U.S. microbiologist has recently stated, through alternative media, that AIDS was developed at Fort Detrick, Maryland, Langley, Virginia, and Wackenhut Laboratories in California, owned by the Hercules Corporation. George Bush is a major stock holder in that company.

"This same microbiologist stated that, through genetic engineering, scientists spliced the AIDS virus into small pox and polio vaccines that were given to the masses in Africa. The purpose? Population reduction—a well publicized goal of the New World Order crowd.

Joyce Riley held up a copy of Time magazine. "And what is the U.S. Government saying about the Gulf War? A 1996 article in this magazine states: 'No Gas Used Against the Troops,' the government stated there was no scientific or medical evidence that chemical or biological weapons were deployed at any level. That is an absolute lie. I have proof that they knew that chemical and biological agents were used. Another article from the Washington Times states, 'Pentagon Says There is No Gulf War Disease.'

"The Persian Gulf War Veterans Coordinating Board stated that they contacted every one of us to see if we were sick. Another lie. I have not met one person yet who was contacted.

"I was approached by someone who lead me to Drs. Garth and Nancy Nicholson. They are both Ph.D. scientists at the M.D. Anderson Cancer Center. Their daughter was in the 101st Airborne which went deep into Iraq and she came home ill. She gave the disease to her parents and also to the family cat. The cat died. They tested its blood and their's, and found Mycoplasma Incognitas, which is the chief biological agent responsible for these illnesses.

"Mycoplasma Incognitas can spread through a population, and as long as your immune system is strong, it will not affect you. But, according to the Nicholsons', the scientists who were involved in this horrible plot inserted 40% of the HIV envelope gene into the Mycoplasma. It gives you symptoms similar to HIV. So, they realized that they had a warfare germ on their hands. It is the first biological agent identified, and there are others.

"The Nicholsons' found that an antibiotic called Doxycycline was the most effective treatment. Tetracycline, readily available from a farmer's coop, is essentially the same. Also, Cipro has been found effective. Other treatments are Ciprofloxacin and Azithromycin. None of these medicines are a total cure and should be administered by a doctor. Building the immune system is a must, with organically grown raw food and juices. Colloidal silver treatments show promise. These remedies are important for us to know as these diseases continue to spread through our communities.

"I received a call from a Special Forces commander who had been retired for one year. He said, 'I served my country. I sent my blood to Dr. Nicholson for free testing and got my prescription for Doxycycline. I went to have it filled and not only did they take away my military ID card, but they would not allow me to have the Doxycycline to save my life.' Would someone please tell me why?

"The disease is contagious, and now the vets' wives and children are getting it. It is going to affect you in the general population. And it is not just in the United States, it is a worldwide problem.

"The early symptoms of the syndrome are deceptive. If you go to your doctor and say, 'I have aching joints or 'chronic fatigue', or you say, 'I don't have the memory I used to,' they will not help you. They have been told there is no Gulf War illness, that it's psychological. In advanced memory loss, vets had to wear beepers so their family could find them. One young man told me, 'I can only remember today. I can't remember what happened yesterday.' He is 27 years old.

"Any Gulf War veteran who has the Mycoplasma knows about night sweats. You have to change your linens twice a night. Muscle spasms get so bad you can't stand it and you scream in pain. There is also loss of eyesight, breathing problems, and chest pains because the Mycoplasma settles in the atrium of the heart.

"Also, you are not being told about the babies who are born deformed. There is a Gulf War Baby Foundation to register babies who have contracted the syndrome. According to 'Nation Magazine,' studies show that 67% of babies born to Gulf War veterans are deformed. What have they done to our future generations? What have they done to their DNA?

"There was an article that appeared in Life Magazine in November, 1995, featuring a man in the 82nd Airborne at Fort Bragg, North Carolina. This young man has a child without arms and legs. I know a nurse in San Antonio who knows of 50 Gulf War children like this. When our soldiers risked their lives in the Gulf, they never imagined that their children would face these consequences, or that their country would turn its back on them. There is no way these parents can afford to take care of these children.

"Some 697,000 active duty service members and 180,000 national guard went to the Gulf. 489,000 of them have since separated from the military. Ask yourself, why, in an all-volunteer force, after a war, would 50% of the individuals involved get out of the military? The reason is they had to, because they were sick and were forced out. To date, the VA reports that more than 489,000 Gulf War veterans have received medical care in VA facilities. One out of every two.

"A letter from Chief of Staff, Shalikashvilli, and Secretary William Perry, dated May 24, 1994, states: 'There have been reports in the press of the possibility that some of you were exposed to biological weapons agents. There is no information, classified or unclassified, that indicates that chemical or biological weapons were used in the Persian Gulf.'

"Well, I'm sorry. There is plenty of evidence. It has already been presented on the floor of the Senate, as the Reigle Report, entitled, 'Is Military Research Hazardous to Veterans Health?' Dated December 8, 1994. This is something that the government does not want you to know. Senator Reigle from Michigan is a brave man, but he is no longer in the Senate. He said, 'I am deeply troubled that the United States permitted the sale of deadly biological agents to a country with a known biological warfare program.' He also stated, 'the Department of Defense refuses to acknowledge the problem. Their blanket denials are not credible. To my mind, there is no more serious crime than an official military cover-up of facts that could prevent more effective diagnosis and treatment of sick U.S. veterans.'"

Joyce Riley paused to let that sink into the hearts of her audience who sat silently transfixed.

"This information was known to every senator in office in 1994. Why aren't they doing something about it. Why weren't you told about it?

"I have a classified document that is part of the Chemical-Biological log that belonged to General Norman Schwarkopf. It is sort of a roadmap of the war and what transpired. It states: 'Colonel Dunn has confirmed that the soldiers of the 3rd AD have blisters, characteristic of mustard chemical agent, on upper and lower arms.' Remember the official statement? 'No Biological or Chemical Weapons Used.' The log continues, 'Arcent advised that casualties happened on afternoon of 28 February, a reddening of the skin and small blisters.'

"I spoke to several of the Medivac flight nurses who accompanied the troops out of the theater of operations. They told me many of the men had severe skin damage, evidence of chemical burn. Autopsies done at Dover, Delaware, found that some of the deaths were due to chemical poisoning.

"Schwarkopf's log continues, 'Msgt Blue called. Subject: Commander's Guidance for Disposition of captured chemical and biological munitions.' Field destruction is OK, but bulk destruction may have international implications.'

"I also want everyone to know that many of our veterans' medical files are missing, possibly destroyed in the Oklahoma City bombing. An attorney actually was sent to prison for destroying veterans medical records. The proof of many of those who received vaccinations is also missing.

"What about the mainstream news media? They have generally ignored the evidence or supported the government's position. The Kansas City Star, on October 14th, read, 'Iraq lied to us about having and using biological weapons.' You know as well as I do that we have satellites in the sky that enable us to see what the Iraqis' are having for dinner. Besides, our people knew Hussein had germ agents because they sold them to him.

"The media is going to have to deal with Gulf War illness because so many people have it now. Dr. Nicholson told me that 20% of the people around the theater of operations, United Arab Emirates, Bahrain, etc. are sick. It is coming to a place near you, believe me. I received a call from a doctor the other day who said that he has 15 patients with Chronic Fatigue Syndrome who didn't know anyone who went to the Gulf War. It's transmissible through sex and kissing, because Mycoplasma is now showing up in the dental floss test.

"'An article in 'Scientific American,' October, 1995, wants you to believe that we will soon be having incredible viruses all over the world, apparently for no reason at all. Many biologists are saying that they never heard of any of these viruses before. How many of you ever heard of the Hantavirus, or Ebola, or Chronic Fatigue before the Gulf War?

"'Scientific American' tells us, 'the primary cause of most cases of hemorragic fever is ecological disruption resulting from human activity.' In other words, we cut down too many trees in the rain forest and those bugs are going to get us. I've never heard of hemorragic fever viruses and I've been a nurse for 25 years, but some of the Gulf War illnesses contain these viruses. Gulf War veterans have told me they are bleeding from every part of their body. It is similar to the Ebola virus, but takes two years to kill.

"The media never told you that George Bush was almost brought up before a Grand Jury. He was subpoenaed in an illegal export case that involved shipment of biological agents to Iraq. In 1993, the Justice Department said he didn't have to honor the subpoena. He was also brought up before a war crimes tribunal. You didn't know about that either, right? Get the book by Ramsey Clark.

"'Media Bypass' magazine, which is definitely not mainstream, stated: 'The buildup of Iraq's weapons was paid for by U.S. taxpayers, and this business was conducted for years before the Persian Gulf War, and after it started. Such trading with the enemy is tantamount to treason. Because Iraq defaulted on payment for the biological agents received from U.S. companies, American taxpayers ended up stuck with the bill for weapons that were later used against coalition forces.'

"Part of the reason it was covered up is that President Bush's father was involved in the Brown Brothers Harriman Bank, which dealt with the transactions.

"How was this cover-up of the manufacture of weapons for Iraq handled in the United States? Bush arranged for 70% of the policy-makers in the Department of Justice to remain in their jobs when Clinton was elected. The official stance from the Justice Department is, 'we cannot talk about this because the independent prosecutor has said, through the courts, that no one is to discuss this investigation officially, until it is finished.'

"Few people know that George Bush's father, Prescott Bush, and the Rockefellers, materially and financially, supported the buildup of Nazi Germany, and later Communist Russia, to create International Socialism.

"Information on Gulf War diseases was sent to President Clinton in 1994. He then started a 'Presidential Advisory Task Force.' Which is a whitewash and cover-up. The Task Force people called me and asked, 'can you tell us what you think is causing the Gulf War illness?' I said, 'it doesn't make any difference what I think. Twelve thousand troops are already dead, and you need to be finding out why. We all know why—biological and chemical agents.' They said, 'well, we can't pinpoint exactly what virus or bacteria is causing the problem, so we can't treat it.' I said, 'you say you don't know what causes cancer, but you treat that!' It is amazing that they are taking this stance, dragging their feet, and trying to make the Gulf War vets feel that it is their fault. They give them psychotropic drugs, or try to buy them off with a 10% disability, $89 per month, which makes them feel like they are getting something they deserve.

"If Saddam Hussein had wanted to kill our soldiers, he would have just outright killed them with mustard or cyanide, right? That wasn't the plan. The plan was to give them a long-term illness that they would bring back to their families. What better way to spread a disease than to give it to the military that moves all over the country?

"I believe the reasons for the Gulf War were threefold. First, to infect the U.S. military, and subsequently, the U.S. and world population. Secondly, to reacquire Kuwait oil fields, most of which are owned by a well-known family in London. And thirdly, to test weaponry on Iraq. Part of the cover-up involves George Bush and members of his administration who held stock in some of the biotech companies that produced biologicals shipped to Iraq. Another part of the cover-up involves a company known as U.S. Arms, which sold Iraq conventional weapons. Ron Brown, who was in the aircraft that was blown up in Bosnia, was on the board of Directors of U.S. Arms. Four individuals on the plane were to testify in an upcoming hearing. Traces of thermite, denoting explosives, were found on the bodies. President Clinton recently claimed 'executive privilege' as reason for not disclosing certain documents to Congress relating to arms shipments to Iraq. Do you understand, yet?

"Important people are being protected by the Department of Defense and the Veterans Administration —people who profited personally from the arms and biologicals trade with Saddam. Besides George Bush, ex-Secretary of State, James Baker III, and Baker's former Under Secretary of Defense and now Clinton's Director of the CIA, John Deutch, should be investigated by Congress for violation of the Trading with the Enemy Act.

"Admission of chemcial/biological warfare, as well as the U.S. biologicals sales to Saddam, would also be very embarrassing for General Colin Powell, General Schwartzkoph, and other top generals who obviously knew about this and lied to America.

"Lies always beget more lies. If the Department of Defense and VA admit that Gulf War Illness exists, the entire cover-up of biological sales to Saddam, our inadequate preparations, perhaps our use of biologicals against Saddam, and their whole edifice of lies over the past five years would unravel, and we would be looking at the greatest scandal in American history —dwarfing Whitewater, Watergate, Teapot Dome and all others put together.

"We have to spread the word to mainstream America. I would ask you to contact your Congressman and your newspapers. You need to see a letter from your Senator either admitting or denying all of this. If he was in office in 1994, he knows about the Reigle Report.

"In closing, I want to say that the sick veterans need your prayers, as do my dear husband, Dave, who has been such a big help, and myself. I am only here as a messenger. I am just one person that is not going to be quiet. I am not going to let our Gulf War veterans die and suffer without Americans knowing what happened to them. Thank you all so very much."

Joyce Riley closed her portfolio and quietly resumed her seat. Normally, Pastor Dixon would have returned to the pulpit to close the service, but not this night. A solemn hush now filled the church as most of the members sat with heads bowed and several sobbed softly. After long moments, a subdued male voice in the rear prayed for Joyce Riley, followed by an elderly lady's tearful prayer for her grandson who had just joined the Air Force.

This impromptu prayer meeting lasted to well past midnight, and when Joyce Riley had finally finished her good-byes and was almost to her car, a good looking man about thirty approached her.

"Excuse me, Ma'am," he said, holding out a card. My name is Carmen DeFaglio. I just want you to know my friends and I are behind you one hundred percent."

"Where you from?" Joyce Riley asked, accepting the card.

"I'm with the 'Watchmen' militia of southern Illinois, near Marion. A few of us came over here tonight to hear you speak. Some of our guys are vets and aren't doing too well. Your talk tonight will be a big help. "I really want to thank you. These guys have no idea where to go for help—the VA gives them Prozac and a slap on the back."

"Well, thanks, but the credit goes to the Lord. He's the one pushing me and gives me the strength to keep going."

"I know what you mean," Carmen agreed.

"You're the first militia person I've met," Joyce Riley said. "Aren't you suppose to have a shaved head and swastika tattoos?"

"Right. And don't forget the assortment of automatic weapons I have stashed everywhere in my Dodge compact."

They both laughed. Then Carmen said, "Seriously, we're just a bunch of guys from all backgrounds that are fed up with corrupt government. Actually, I'm from Chicago, but I joined the outfit in southern Illinois 'cause its the best one around. We were raided recently by the ATF and FBI on bogus charges so we meet secretly. I lost my best friend in that raid—Scott White. He tried to be a peace maker and they blew his brains out. But they can't stop us because we've drawn the line. It's either that or slavery."

"That's sad about your friend, but maybe his death wasn't in vain. We only see dimly now, you know."

"That's right, you never know."

"Do you have many women participating in your group?

"Quite a few. We call them the kitchen militia. Their weapons are telephones and computers and their ammunition is information. We think we've got to educate everyone while we're still able to."

"You got that right. Those of us who have been given truth need to be faithful in passing it on to those who are open. Keep up the good work."

They parted then, and neither noticed the man in the pickup parked two cars over. His window was down and he had listened to their conversation. After they left, he sat there in the shadows, thinking about them and the things he had heard that evening. Beside him on the seat was a note pad he had planned to use to copy license numbers in the parking lot. But somehow, he never got to it, nor did he use the tape recorder concealed in his jacket to record the meeting. After a while, he started up his truck and drove back to his motel.

On Tuesday, Zoe was back at his St. Louis desk and halfheartedly writing a makeshift report for Barrows. Joyce Riley's stinging presentation blazed in his mind, and it was all he could do to not announce to the office staff that the government they worked for had deliberately caused the suffering and death of thousands of veterans.

As winter approached, he stayed in St. Louis during the week and drove to the farm each weekend. He began drinking again, in the St. Louis bars at night, and the entire weekend at home. He had a hard time sleeping, having almost total recall of raids he had taken part in against gun dealers who were often found to be operating legally after further investigation. And now, he appreciated the mental duress they must have suffered.

He thought about the children burned alive at Waco, Weaver's wife, shot through the head, holding her baby. Hauntingly, he recalled those who had lost their lives more recently because of him—particularly the zealot holding the cross, and a girl with big eyes and silver blond hair under a fatigue cap, and he wondered how he could justify working for the government any longer. But what would he do, stay on the farm, stock pile food and wait for the calamity supposedly soon to come?

One Friday morning in late January of 1996, he was summoned to Barrow's office. He was surprised to find FBI agent Harding standing at the window when he entered the room. Barrows sat at his desk, studying some photos. When he looked up, Zoe could tell he wasn't very happy.

"Hello, John," Harding said, sticking out a hand and clicking on his political smile. "It's been a long time."

"To be sure."

"Desk work got to you yet?"

"That's putting it mildly."

"Well, maybe we can do something about that."

Barrows cleared his throat. "John, the FBI is requesting your assistance in a—"

"We've got a problem out west that Washington wants us to take care of," Harding interrupted. "One of those patriot freaks, a Jack Koontz, from Midland, Texas, took some county officials to court over a land title fight. Supposedly, while he was doing research to prepare his case, he discovered that an 1845 treaty annexing Texas to the United States was never properly ratified, meaning Texas is still what it was back then, an independent Republic.

"He and his people have set up their own government, common law courts, the works. They claim the Federal government has no jurisdiction on Texas soil. They even filed a commercial lien under UCC and ICC treaties on 393,000 square miles of Texas land, claiming eminent domain."

"Can they get away with that?" Zoe asked.

"Evidently. According to our legal people, a perfected lien is recognized as an international asset and, indeed, can be sold on the open market. And that's exactly what they're doing, they've already received a large payment. To make matters worse, they've served a notice to vacate on German companies and troops training in Texas. They claim they're trespassing."

"What's he really after?" Zoe asked.

"He demands that Texans be given the chance to vote whether or not to stay under Federal jurisdiction, or be recognized as an independent nation. Personally, I think he's trying to set up his own little kingdom."

"A vote can't hurt anything, there's no way most Texans will buy his program."

Harding smiled. "I should tell you there are similar movements already started in Colorado and Hawaii."

"Somewhat reminiscent of what happened to the Soviet Union and its satellite countries," Barrows said.

"Well, Washington doesn't think it will get that far," Harding answered. "They thought he was a joke, then people became very nervous when those liens got bought up by investors. There are other ramifications, too, I don't have time to go into it now. My orders are to defuse the situation without delay. The plan is uncomplicated. Cut off the head and the body will die." Harding reached for the photos on Barrow's desk. "Take a look at these. Koontz is on the last one."

They were aerial shots of a ranch in the center of a large desert valley, surrounded by foothills, totally in the open.

"Last week, Koontz disappeared from Midland. Luckily, we were able to plant Global Position Systems transponders on his vehicles while he was still there. We tracked him by satellite to this remote ranch near the border of New Mexico. As you can tell, he is really out in the open. That first rise there that's been marked is at least 1,200 yards from the house."

"So that's where I come in."

"We don't have anyone else who can hold a candle to you in long distance work, or has your experience in concealment in open country."

"I take it all negotiations have failed."

"Of course. His answer was the liens. He refuses to respond to the warrants against him. Our information is he went to this place because he's far less accessible there and plans to make a stand. Number of people with him is undetermined, there can't be more than a dozen, or so."

"What about the Texas militia?"

"We think they're all talk, but that shouldn't be a problem if we move clandestinely now. Above all, Washington does not want a long term standoff like Waco with all the publicity. We have a brief window of opportunity while the media is still deaf and dumb.

Zoe found a photo of a good looking slender guy dressed in a well fitted business suit, too young to be partially bald. He was drawn to the gentle expression in the guy's face.

"Does Washington really believe taking this guy out will solve anything? I've seen these patriots up close—they're not going away."

"We think you should use a spotter," Harding said, obviously ignoring that remark.

Zoe didn't answer, he just kept looking at the guy's face.

Finally he said, "Out of the question."

"Oh, why?"

"Another man just increases the chance of being seen. The reason you want me is that I know *how* to do it. So let me do it my way."

"Still the hard case. All right. How soon can you leave?"

"Let me think about it over the weekend."

Harding looked quickly at Barrows. "Is there a problem?"

Zoe thought about it. "You're asking me to take out a guy for purely political reasons."

"What the hell were you doing over in Vietnam behind enemy lines, if it wasn't that?" Harding snapped angrily.

"A lot of stuff I was asked to do, I did because I was a green kid who didn't know better. We were told everybody with slant eyes was the enemy and we were at war."

Harding calmed down. "Okay. Just understand that if this movement ever got out of hand it could ruin the nation. Washington is fuming." He began to put on his top coat. "I'm overdue for a meeting and I haven't got time to philosophize. Here's your chance to get back into action, but if you decide not to, maybe desk work is a better choice, now that you're getting older."

Zoe got the message.

Harding started out the door, then paused. "If this job is done cleanly, there's a $5,000 bonus in it as an expression of gratitude from the Administration." And he walked out.

Zoe drove to the farm right from the office, and that night, he lay in the bedroom of his youth under three comforters and listened to the old farmhouse creak and shudder from the howling wind. Anxiety and indecision clung to him like a leech. *Where are you now, Dad? You always had such good advice. I should have listened more.*

Once, long ago, he thought he heard hushed voices calling him back to a peaceful valley in a distant land, indeed, in the dark of night, or was it in a dream, that he felt his soul plead to return from where he had come, perhaps in the beginning. But he had no memory of a *beginning*—only a valley, the Kerayan, but a mere wisp of fantasy now. And in its place, his life, a crazy quilted patchwork of color here or there, but making no sense at all except for the one absolute—death.

He lay a long time into the night hearing the wind, and then he began to really *listen* to the wind, to a whisper in the wind, or was it something from long ago. But there was no mistaking the message—*always listen to your heart, son, it won't lie to you.*

Saturday morning he was up before sunrise. He selected two of his best rifles, 1000 rounds of match grade ammo, and an assortment of scopes. He dug out camping gear and other survival items and crammed everything into the Corvette.

Then he went to the kitchen and found a writing pad and a large manila envelope and wrote a letter of resignation. He put it and his credentials in the envelope and addressed it to Barrows.

Taking one last fond look around the old place, he got into the Corvette and drove west—to a place in Texas close to New Mexico where a line had been drawn in the sand and his help was badly needed.

End

Epilogue

I had a dream the other night that I really
didn't understand,
a figure walked in through the mist with a
flintlock in his hand.
His clothes were torn and dirty as he
stood there by my bed,
he took off his three-cornered hat and
speaking low to me he said,

We fought a revolution to secure our liberties,
we wrote the Constitution as a shield
from tyranny.
For future generations this legacy we gave,
in this, the land of the free and
home of the brave.

The freedoms we secured for you we hoped
you'd always keep,
the tyrants labored endlessly while your
parents were asleep.
Your freedoms' gone, your courage lost,
you're no more than a slave, in this,
the land of the free and home of the brave.

You buy permits to travel and permits
to own a gun,
permits to start a business, or to build
a place for one—

On the land that you believe you own
but pay yearly rent, although you have no
voice in saying how the money's spent.

Your children must attend a school that
doesn't educate,
and your Christian values can't be taught
according to the State.
You read about the current news in a
regulated press,
and you pay a tax you do not owe to please
the IRS.

Your money is no longer made of
silver nor of gold,
you trade your wealth for paper so your life
can be controlled.
You pay for crimes that make our nation
turn from God in shame,
you've taken Satan's number and traded in
your name.

You've given government control to those
who do you harm,
so they can burn down churches and seize
the family farm.
And keep our country deep in debt, put
men of God in jail,
harass your fellow countrymen, while
corrupted courts prevail.

Your public servants don't uphold the
solemn oath they've sworn,
and your daughters visit doctors so their
children won't be born.
Your leaders send artillery and guns to
foreign shores,
and send your sons to slaughter fighting
other peoples' wars.

Can you regain the freedom for which
we fought and died,
or don't you have the courage or faith
to stand with pride?
And are there no more values for which
you'll fight to save?
Or do you wish your children to live
in fear and be slaves?

Oh sons of the Republic, arise, take a stand,
defend the Constitution,
the Supreme law of the land.
Preserve our great Republic and each
God-given right,
and pray to God to keep the torch of freedom
burning bright.

As I awoke, he vanished in the mist
from which he came,
his words were true—we are not free,
but we have ourselves to blame.

For even now, as tyrants trample each
God-given right,
we only watch and tremble, too afraid
to stand and fight.

If he stood by your bedside in a dream
while you were asleep,
and wondered what remains of the freedoms
he fought to keep.
What would be your answer
if he called out from the grave—
Is this still the land of the free and home
of the brave?

God Bless you and God bless this Republic.

A Visitation From The Past,
a song by Steve Vaus.

ACKNOWLEDGMENTS

The author wishes to thank the following persons and organizations for providing certain critical information included in this book.

Texe Marrs	*Circle of Intrigue*
Dave and Joyce Riley	Gulf War Veterans Assoc. Phone: 713-438-1699
Colonel Daniel Marvin	U.S. Spec. Forces (Retired)
Dr. Greg Dixon	Indianapolis Baptist Temple
Thalen Paulk	Songwriter
Mr. Sea	Investigator
Tom Robinson	Investigator
Johnny Johnson	Texas Militia
Media Bypass	Magazine
Clayton Douglas	*Free American* Newspaper
"Michael" Journal	Magazine
Cherith Chronicle	Magazine
World Colony News	*Magazine*